David Oyekunle

# FOR WHEN STARS ALIGN

Lightleaf

Printed in Lagos, Nigeria by Lightleaf Publishers

FOR WHEN STARS ALIGN


ISBN: 978-978-787-921-4

A catalogue record of this book is available from the National Library of Nigeria.

*To the dreamers reaching for their dreams,*
*it is possible.*

# CONTENTS

# WHY WAS THIS BOOK WRITTEN?

In the heart of Lagos, where dreams are as diverse as the bustling streets, an anecdote unfolds about the power of resilience and the magic of perseverance. "For When Stars Align," charts the journey of a boy whose beginnings were as humble as they were challenging, transforming a story of survival into one of spectacular success.

Intelligence without ambition is like a bird without wings!

This book is an odyssey that begins with a young dreamer, navigating through the dense fog of adversity with nothing but a wheelbarrow and a pocket full of dreams. It's a narrative that resonates deeply with anyone standing at the crossroads of potential and opportunity, offering not just inspiration, but a blueprint for navigating the journey from aspiration to achievement.

In essence, it's more than just a story; it's an echo of the universal pursuit of greatness. It tells the tale of transforming meagre beginnings into a life of abundance through sheer will and determination. For When Stars Align is rich with imagery that evokes a sense of journey and discovery; it's a mentor, and a friend for those who dare. It encourages readers to keep their aspirations alive and reassures them that in the tapestry of life, every challenge, every setback, and every triumph is a star waiting to align for their ultimate success. The book explores timeless themes of resilience and belief, highlighting how taking action can lead to achieving one's highest aspirations, regardless of life's ups and downs.

# THE VISIONARY CANVAS

"Oliver! Oliver!"

The voice called. It was a familiar voice. It rang above the noise of the street he was walking in. On any other day, he would have crossed the busy road and gone over for some chit-chat, but not that day. He had other things on his mind. Important things that could not wait.

So he worked up a smile, turned his face towards the direction the voice came from, and waved his hand above the sea of cars on the road that separated him and the greeter and continued walking.

He could feel the disappointment from across the road, but that didn't deter his determined strides.

"Not today, John. What has all our chit-chat gotten us?" He muttered under his breath and continued walking.

He had only walked for a few minutes when he heard his name again.

"Oliver!"

Oliver shook his head and wondered why people kept calling him, but he knew that was his price for being famous. It was his price for being the barrow boy.

"Oliver!" the person called again.

It came from behind him. It was not familiar, but frankly, he did not care. He was not in the state of mind for unending jest and chat that led and contributed to nothing.

This time, he did not look back nor acknowledge the greeting. He kept on his determined strides.

Oliver.

His name. His God-given name like his mother loves to add, with a warm smile.

Oliver, the bane of many teases and hopes.

The memories came rushing in and he drifted...

It was at his cousin's wedding party. Aunty Audrey had lived with his mother for some years before she secured admission to the university. So, there was a history, and the benefit of that was that his mother got to meet Aunty Audrey's husband before the rest of the extended family. Another benefit was that Oliver's mother and her immediate family get to be treated specially at the wedding party. It was not demanded, it was not alluded to in conversations. It was just expected. Like an unspoken societal rule that was expected to be adhered to, Oliver milked this advantage well. That day at the wedding party, he kept asking for more plates of rice again and again until the people, his friends at the table, shouted.

A friend, in between laughs, had said "A mother and a father named their child Oliver, what were you expecting? Of course, he would ask for more," and there was more laughter.

Oliver, not ashamed of his ravenous appetite, joined in the laughter. He had nothing against the name then. But time would change that. Life changed it. He was thirteen.

His name is an indication of good things to come, a harbinger of hope.

His father and mother had told him. His teachers in secondary school had said so, especially when he failed to do well in his examinations to their expectations, which was often.

They said his name reminds them of a known fictional character in a book with the same name. Oliver Twist, in that fiction book, not only asked for more food but eventually went on to ask for more in life. Though an unreal person, Oliver Twist left a trail everyone expected him to follow.

Oliver Peterson wished his plea for more could go beyond food. Heck, for years he tried to ask more from life. He tried to get more and be more, he had dreams that he wished he could reach. He dreamt about reaching these dreams, he spoke to anyone who cared to listen about these dreams. Not only did he want to be like this fictional character who, though not living or ever lived, has cast shadows and aspersions upon his life. He wanted to live out the dreams of his heart and be fulfilled.

Yet even this seemingly simple wish had eluded him. Year in and year out, trying as much as he could, he just could not make this wish, this dream of his heart come to pass. It was not for lack of trying, he simply could not find his way out of his misery. So, his thoughts turned black and bleak. He berated everything and everyone, himself the hardest. He even berated Charles Dickens. Sometimes he wished the man was still alive, so he could find him and give him a piece of his mind. His life would have been fine, if he had not written that book with the character that everyone now expects him to model.

Oliver Peterson knew, just like we all know, that when he looks outward for a solution that can only be found within and by adhering to time-proven principles, his anger and blame were misdirected.

In the weeks before he left home, his mother had taken to calling his name at odd times and in odd ways. Like when he was washing clothes or sitting in front of the house, alone, staring into space. The first time she did, he had answered, but she had said nothing. She just stared at him for a few seconds and left. When she did it the second time, Oliver got it. It was a juggling of his memory, as if she was intentionally bringing to his remembrance what his name embodied. The promises it held. The things he should be doing that he was not doing. It was a call to action.

Weeks back, he had sunk into gloom at the enormity of this, wondering if things would ever change. Not any more. Things were about to change. Things would change.

Oliver remembered how he had wanted things to change, how he stoically believed things could change. It was a belief that sprang from the books he had read. He had come to know that desire responds to actions. Taking action was the trigger needed to ignite his dreams. This was what sowed the desire to relocate in his heart. He needed to do something, he had to get a job. There was not so much he could do in his quaint town. He had a desire to build a big business one day, but for that to metamorphose into reality, he needed money. An obscene amount of money that his mother nor any relative couldn't give him. He had just one option; work, and because opportunities were limited in his town, he relocated.

Oliver had tall dreams, dreams which were soon deflated by shocking realities. There were opportunities in the town he relocated to, but they were not easy to come by. They were not easily seen and picked like pebbles on the street like he had been made to believe.

And so, after weeks of painful search and depleted resources, he took up the job of a barrow boy. It was the easiest and fastest job he could get. All he needed was a wheelbarrow and the strength to push. Every morning, just before the sun rose, Oliver would wash his face and feet, and walk the long distance to the market. He would go from one stall to the other in search of customers who needed his wheelbarrow to carry their purchases. He worked from sun up to sun down. He pushed a barrow and made friends. He was diligent and courteous, and was soon nicknamed 'The Barrow Boy'.

He became the go-to carrier for premium customers. He was loved, and his tips were great, but Oliver knew there was more. So, he spent his days thinking of a way of escape. He often turned and tossed at night on the hard, cold floor in the room he shared with six other barrow boys, thinking of a life beyond pushing barrows. He wondered what would become of his aspirations. As he pushed his barrow around the market, he thought of his father, who worked and worked until he slumped under the strain of it. A lifelong barrow boy was not a worthy reward.

When Oliver sweated under the hot sun, he often saw in his mind's eye, his mother doing the same, pushing barrows from one door to the other selling petty things at ridiculous prices. He was stuck in the same rut. It was a realisation he detested.

He was called 'the barrow boy,' but that moniker would change soon. Oliver began to see his time pushing his wheelbarrow as the dry season in his life. A time in life when there was dearth and hardship, when nothing grew and the ones that did were measly. Oliver swore his dreams and desires would live and transcend this dryness. He reiterated to himself that this dry season was part of his journey to becoming. This dryness was not his end, it was not his destination.

He had dreams, and he resolved that they would not be choked by the hotness of the dry season of his life. The fertile ground of his life may not yield fruits now, but Oliver believed a time would come when it would yield plenty. It is possible if he believed things would change. It would change. He needed it to change.

"I am going to..."

"Oli, Oli, Oliver!" Oliver's muttering was suddenly interrupted.

He knew the voice. This one he could not ignore. So he moved towards the voice, he dodged kiosks and trays until he got to her stall. It was Mama Julie, his mother's friend who had also relocated from their quaint town. She sold roasted plantain on some months, and roasted corn the others, whichever was in season.

"Oliver, I have been calling you, hope you are hearing from your mother?" She asked.

"Yes ma, yes ma." He said and rushed through the pleasantries.

When they were done, he got back on track, on the path that would lead him to the first step in reaching for his dreams. He walked faster, more determinedly, his hands unconsciously patting the exercise book rolled into his back pocket, until he got there.

It was a secluded spot near an old oak tree. He loved the seclusion and quiet because it allowed his thoughts to roam without distractions. When he was there, his thoughts often danced like the leaves in the wind, free from all encumbrances. It was the perfect place to paint the canvas of his vision. He brought out the exercise book from his back pocket, took a pen from the pocket on his shirt and sat under the oak tree. He sighed contentedly as a gentle wind blew and rustled the leaves of the tree under which he sat. His heart churned with ideas, his heart seemed to leap within him with joy. The idea of leaving his current predicament and becoming successful echoed in his mind like a sweet melody that promised a harmonious future, and it warmed his heart.

Finally, after all these years, things were about to change for him.

# NAVIGATING CHALLENGES

Oliver was at it again, pushing and pulling a wheelbarrow with all the strength he could muster. His sweat flowed freely like water as he laboured to push, but it was a fatigue that stemmed from a lack of motivation rather than physical stress.

He had woken up that morning tired and angry. He believed in the process, but what happens when the process begins to look as if it would never end? When all the money he hoped he would have gathered after his six months on the job remained nothing but a wish. He had spent six months pushing barrows and he had nothing to show for it but a pair of new shoes and second-hand clothes.

How would he ever get out of this rat race if what he earned was barely enough to feed and clothe him? How would he ever get to achieve the vision nesting between the pages of the exercise book he took to the oak tree? The goals and resolution he made that day seemed like a lifetime away, he wondered if they would ever become a reality, his reality.

Weighed down by these thoughts, Oliver had gone to bed sulking and woken up not an inch better. He pushed himself up reluctantly from his place on the hard and cold floor, hissing and murmuring angrily as he picked his way around the other barrow boys in the cramped room.

In anger, he skipped his morning routine of washing his face and feet and took to the road that led to the market. He kicked pebbles angrily as he walked, hoping and praying one would hurt him so he would have an excuse to not go to work.

The pebbles did not bother him. In fact, he thought they probably loved him. However, everyone at the market kept asking him why he wasn't his usual bubbly and smiling self. In response, he would force a smile and give the one-word answer, "fine."

Everyone was fine with that except this customer, who was determined to get him talking. This woman whose unending efforts at starting a conversation were grating irritatingly on what was left of his good-naturedness. He pushed and pulled her purchase in his wheelbarrow around the market when she said:

"Barrow boy, I was going to say this a long time ago but for the life of me, I don't know why I keep forgetting. I was going to ask if you had any formal education. You talk like an educated man."

Oliver stopped at that. No one had ever asked him that. His heart swelled with joy. It was not about the question, it was what the question meant. That he was seen, that someone saw beyond his rags. Someone paid attention enough to notice that he was different. When he took the barrow job, being different was one of the things he knew would give him an edge, and he did that by talking differently, being courteous and diligent. If people noticed, they did not say, they just nicknamed him 'Barrow Boy' and gave him more jobs and tips.

That was fine, but there was a part of him that yearned for approval and applause, an applause expressed through words. Affirmations that showed he had made and was making a difference, but he did not get it. It seems lay people are less concerned with affirmations and encouraging words.

What use would words be to people who were already downtrodden, so much that the possibilities of their ascension are a lofty reality for their mind to conceive?

Oliver, with all his qualifications, was one of those people. His attempt to show that he was different couldn't change that in his customers' minds. They tossed him his pay and kept their affirming words and observations.

Except for this woman.

"Yes, Ma'am, I am educated. I have a bachelor's degree," Oliver said, overly intentional with his diction and intonation. She noticed. Why not go the whole mile, he reasoned.

"Wow, that is awesome! Are you cool doing this, or would you love a change? Nothing big but definitely better than this. Are you interested?" She asked.

Oliver stared, jaw dropped, and speechless.

It was the same reaction he had when he got a call from her a week later to resume as a factory worker in one of the manufacturing companies in the town.

Oliver started his new job in awe of his good fortune.

Being a factory worker was a far cry from what he hoped to do with his life, but it was better than pushing a wheelbarrow through the market. He had more money now, enough to feed him and to save. He could get his own room and carve out time for his personal development. It looked like the dry, unproductive season of his life was nearing its end. There was a sign of harvest. A rain of abundance was imminent.

***

A few months later, Oliver was sitting in a modest sitting room willing the other occupant, Maurice, would speed things up. Oliver looked at the object of his anger and smiled despite his tumultuous emotions.

Oliver watched Maurice as he gently took one morsel after the other from the bowl in front of him. Typical, gentle Maurice style, it was easy to see him this way and make a conclusion about him, but it would be far from the truth. Maurice's gentility ended with his manners, he was a ferocious goal-setter and risk-taker.

Oliver had been friends with him for two months. It was a friendship that lends truth to the fact that setting goals can change the life of the goal-setter. It changed him and gave him this beautiful friendship.

He met Maurice at the manufacturing company where he works. They were employed on the same day as ground crew workers at the flip-flops manufacturing factory. The ground crew was a conglomeration of young and middle-aged men who worked every day of the week except Sundays. They spent a greater part of the twenty-four hours a day working and looking forward to payday. Then after that payday, the next, and the next and the next after that. It was a never-ending cycle of dependency. Most of them had nothing to look forward to, so they did not care so much for the future, they couldn't even think that far.

"Let us eat and drink today, for tomorrow we die," was an unspoken mantra that most lived by. It was evident in their speech and how they spent the money they made. They lavished their earnings on things with no worthy value, assets with no multiplying effect. It was evident in how they resolved conflicts. Fighting until blood was shed or until someone was injured was a common thing for them. The present was enough. The present was all they cared about.

It was a scary way to live, but it was how these men with all their lives ahead of them lived. Maurice was different, however. He did not say much, but it was obvious to all that he was not interested in settling, his sight was set on more. He spoke like someone that wanted more, he dressed the part. He was working towards more. He worked twice as hard, went after more tasks, was diligent, punctual, and had a good attitude. It was only normal and expected that he would be noticed, and he was. This was to Maurice's fortune but to his fellow ground crew colleagues, chagrin and angst. He got one promotion after another, and now he was just one step away from becoming one of the supervisors.

Oliver and others had seethed with anger and envy at Maurice's progress. They called him all manner of names and gave excuses for his hard work. They said they were sure he knew someone amongst the senior executives who was calling the shots for him.

Sometimes at night, however, in his cramped one-room apartment, on his flatbed, with the light from his kerosene lamp casting a glow in his dark room, Oliver wondered if others knew how intentional Maurice was. His success and climb up the company's administrative ladder was not incidental, it was scripted. Maurice wrote his own success story. He knew the actions that he would take that would get him noticed and put him on the path to success. He wrote and acted out the script. He was still writing it and they, the other ground crew workers, were unwilling spectators.

On one of such nights, he wondered if intentionally chasing goals could help him, too. He wondered if the knowledge he got from books about goals paving the way for success was valid, and if the stories he heard of people who came into success was ever going to be his story too. He began to respect Maurice and imagined what friendship with him would be like.

He moved closer to Maurice to know what his secrets to achieving his dreams and vision were. After narrating to him how he had written down his dreams and visions but didn't know how to pull them off, Maurice shared with him a key ingredient to achieving one's dreams and aspirations, and what Oliver was missing; Goal Setting.

Oliver had read about goal setting in books, but he never paid much attention to it, he even thought it was a chore. After his conversation with Maurice, Oliver decided to give his dreams a chance by setting goals. He read some books and attended some seminars on goal setting, then he paid another visit to his quiet spot by the Oak tree.

Now that he had seen the light, he wondered why he had been expecting success all these years when he had failed to do the necessary thing that would ensure it: to have a well-crafted goal. He learnt that behind every successful endeavour lay a well-crafted goal.

It was such a simple and profound truth, yet he had missed it.

His life was a fertile field, a landscape of endless possibilities. There was a purpose for his life, a purpose that only he could birth with corresponding actions like setting goals.

He envisioned his future as a canvas waiting for the brushstrokes of intention to bring it to life. A goal, he thought, would be the palette of colours to paint the masterpiece of his dreams. A well crafted goal was all that was needed to make his life a masterpiece, a beauty that could not be ignored.

As Oliver bent his head and brought pen to paper, he

heard...

"Goooaaal!!!!"

His interest was piqued. Football was his thing, and it seemed a "set match" was going on somewhere, he would have gone to look for where the noise came from and enjoy a beautiful game of football, but he did not. He would not because he knows the allure of distractions.

The distractions of the world often tugged at his attention. The allure of promises that led astray whispered to him like a mischievous wind. But thank goodness for goals. A goal is like a vaccine that wages war and provides immunity against the ills of distractions; it stands as a sentinel guarding and protecting against the pitfalls of distractions.

One of the books he read said that goals are like a guiding star that would provide the direction he needs in the constellation of his desires. Distractions are destructive, they are clogs in the wheels of actualising visions.

What is a man without a vision; without something to look forward to or envision?

"Without a vision, we are rudderless and aimless," he mused, realising that the roadmap of goals is the compass steering him through the vast sea of life. With a goal, he could climb the heights of his aspirations like a ladder, each step a triumph over distractions.

Oliver knew the secret to making something of his

life was to shun distractions and give attention to his goals squarely. He remembered the event he attended a week ago, where one of the speakers had made a profound statement that had taken up space in his heart. As he sat under the cool shade of the oak tree, warding off distractions, the word resounded in his heart: 'Your life is your goal and your goal is your life.'

Simple but powerful, the statement showed that the success he hoped to make of his life, and the story he desired to write of his life were intertwined with his goals. His life was his goal and his goal was his life. Oliver mused over this again as he gave his attention back to the exercise book on his lap.

He would not give in to distractions, he thought and vowed again as he wrote down his first goal.

He looked at what he had written, and his body tingled over with happiness. It was a response to the fact that he was on his way to greater things, better days. It was also a realisation of how intertwined his vision and goals were. It also showed how connected his goals were to his dreams becoming a reality.

Oliver looked at what he had written again, he smiled, rested his head against the trunk of the oak tree and closed his eyes. He saw them, figments of his imagination embracing reality. Dreams accepting life. Visions embodied in tangible things. He saw them all, they were no longer distant mirages but tangible aspirations, waiting for the wings of goals to give them flight. He knew beyond doubt that God's blessings were often intricately woven into purposeful plans, it was a divine design that unfolded with setting goals.

An action he had just taken.

Oliver resumed writing, putting down one carefully written goal after the other in his exercise book, joy bubbled in him as he continued writing, but then he stopped.

In the quietude of the oak tree's shade, Oliver paused, a moment of reflection suspended in time. A moment of reflection borne out of knowledge and understanding. He realized that all the goals he had written were futile if they were not SMART.

Maurice told him about the SMART principle during one of their conversations in his house one hot afternoon as they drank cold soft drinks from glass cups. He told him that goals are meant to be set with time.

"Set with time?" he had asked, and he shed more light on the SMART principle.

He said the SMART principle is an acronym for the words Specific, Memorable, Achievable, Realistic, and Timely—these were the ingredients to give his dreams the needed shine.

This principle holds a promise of fulfilment for the goals he had written. This principle will ensure that his vision, propelled by his goals, sees the light of day. It was a principle every goal-setter should live by.

Every goal is a strategy, a deliberate step toward a specific intended result. Thus, there is a need to be specific. The goal should not be a cluster of vague statements or objectives, it has to be specific, clear, plain, and simple. Specificity, he realised, was the key, it is a guiding star illuminating the path toward fulfilment.

The goal must also be Measurable. The measurability of a goal is not in how bogus the goal is or how it sounds, rather it is in its significance to the realisation of the overall vision. There has to be a yardstick to determine progress, to make sure that one is still on track with the set goals.

The grandeur of benefits that setting goals bring should never make one set goals that are not achievable. The A in the SMART principle stands for Achievable. The goals must be ones that the goal-setter can put his hands on and achieve. The goal-setter must have the wherewithal, capabilities, and ability to bring the goals to pass.

This then brings to the fore, why the goals must be realistic. It is true that faith can make the impossible possible and God delights in the extraordinary. But it is also a known truth that there are set principles that should never be contravened, or else frustration and gloom sets in. The goal setter must be realistic, the goal setter must come to terms with the reality that surrounds and might influence his goals. Knowledge of this prepares and equips him to set goals that would work.

It has to be Timely. It has to be bound to time, to a timeline, a deadline. This is essential as time can be easily stolen by the thief called Procrastination.

Much like the rhythm of the seasons, Oliver recognised the importance of goal-setting calendars —daily, weekly, or monthly structures that would shape his journey.

Maurice also told him that purpose weaved its way through all of his adventures in life as he set goals and worked towards crushing them. Oliver was also an adventurer in the journey of purpose and successful life.

As the young adventurer set his first goal in the serene backdrop of nature, he felt the glory within him stirring and embraced the unfolding journey, eager to impact the pages of his history. He closed the exercise book he had written his goals in and stared ahead. Destiny was summoning him, and he was determined to become the Oliver who accomplished more in life.

***

Now, Maurice was picking his teeth with a toothpick as he just finished a meal.

"Oliver, what were you saying? I am sorry I took your time, you know I don't rush my things." He pointed to the empty bowls in front of him.

"Of course, you don't, you are only ferocious at crushing your goals." Oliver wanted to say, instead he said. "So I have set my goals, ensuring to use the SMART principle. My goals have opened my eyes to see time and opportunities. I am intentional about who comes into my circle as friends, what next?"

Maurice smiled and nodded his head as if he was satisfied about the direction of the question.

"Permit me to start with the question of a renowned man. He said, "Suppose a man wants to build a tower. Will he not first sit down and estimate the cost to see if he has enough money to complete it? For if he lays the foundation and is not able to finish it, everyone who sees it will ridicule him, saying, 'This fellow began to build and was not able to finish'. The same is true about a man who sets goals and does not take into account what that goal will cost him," Maurice concluded.

Oliver nodded his head in agreement to show that he was listening and understood what was said.

Maurice smiled and continued, "Enthusiasm about setting goals is good, but you will need more than that to navigate the complexities of goals actualisation. There must be a careful examination of the conditions, costs, and values associated with each endeavour, with each goal. Oliver, my friend, you see, people are fond of explaining away success but I tell you, behind every glory and every successful goal are stories. Stories of sleepless nights, of hard work, determination, and resilience. These are some of the character traits that must sums the life of a successful goal-setter They must become his companions on this journey to purpose and fulfilment."

Maurice paused to clear his plates, when he came back, he asked Oliver if he understood everything he had said.

"Yes, yes, please continue." Oliver responded.

"Good, let me give you another example. I once heard a speaker say that knowing what the pursuit of your goals will cost you can also be likened to a businessman who starts a business venture after a thorough examination of the capital, risks, profits, and losses. I'll add that, the costs are often not just monetary; they also extend to the challenges that lay ahead. Knowing what price and cost a goal would have you pay will help you in fortifying and preparing yourself for the unexpected twists and turns. It will help you to face challenges squarely."

"So setting goals and counting the cost does not absolve one from challenges?" Oliver asked.

"Of course, it does not! What it does is to arm you with the knowledge to forge ahead in spite of the challenges. It helps to strengthen your resolve and helps you navigate the challenging times and periods successfully. Challenges are not bad in themselves, they are an opportunity and avenue for growth. Challenges reveal to us what we are made of, it reveals our weaknesses and our strengths. It is during a challenging time that most people evolve and become the stars that they are. Challenges should not be avoided, it behoves great benefits for anyone that will stay the course till the end. It is in the furnace of challenges that we are sometimes changed. Challenges also give us the chance to refine our goals. It helps us to take note of things that work and the ones that would not, no matter how much we try. Challenges bring clarity to goals."

As Maurice spoke, Oliver's heart and mind eyes went on a journey, putting pictures to what he was hearing. He saw the pitfalls he had experienced, the obstacles he had faced and how each obstacle had taught him and made him a better person and goal setter. It had made him evolve, it had taught him resilience and determination and to be observant. The masterpiece that was his life could become a reality because he had achieved his goals, faced the challenges, and had become ten times better than when he started. He knew Maurice was right. Like most of his mentors who had taught on goals setting were.

"This applies to all categories of goal, be it short, mid or long term goal." Maurice continued.

"Okay."

"Did I answer your questions?"

Oliver smiled and nodded his head in affirmation.

Maurice had not only answered his questions, he had helped make the roadmap to his goals clear. The road to his goals was a path waiting to be tread and now he had the light and wisdom to tow this path successfully bereft of loss and casualties.

That is the beauty of having mentors, and companions who had gone ahead, and had done some of the things he just started doing, around. They give wisdom and directions to navigate the less trodden path successfully. They point out landmarks and potholes, hold your hands and provide support. They make the journey of purpose worthwhile and less cumbersome.

The pursuit of the goal phase was a journey that demanded courage and foresight. These are some of the things mentors and like-minded companions provide. They speak faith and courage into the goal-setter's heart in times of despair, and give uncommon insight borne out of their experience. Happy is the man who finds these people and submits to learn from them and glean from their wisdom. Just as he was learning from his friend, Maurice.

The ship of his goals was about to set sail once again and as Oliver set the sail towards his aspirations, he carried the words of Myles Munroe in his heart and mulled over it: "A life without a sense of purpose is meaningless."

His life had taken on new meaning from the day he decided to set goals and take intentional actions that would take him closer to his purpose rather than farther from it. He was focused, driven, and ready to take on the world. There was no stopping him now. Things were changing. He heaved a sigh of relief and looked at his friend who had resumed picking his teeth gently with the toothpick.

Thank God for purpose driven friends, he thought, and thanked Maurice for his time and wisdom.

# SCRIPTING SUCCESS

One evening after a hectic day at work, Oliver sat on his bed and went deep in his thoughts. He was in his quaint town again, a lanky thirteen years old boy taking one reluctant step after the other on the path that led to the town's secondary school. He had an unexplained disdain for school. School was not really his cup of tea. There was a time it used to be but things changed. Or better put, he changed.

If he was asked, he would have mentioned a lot of things like how his grades were poor or how some of the teachers rushed through their lessons or how some of the teachings sounded boring and monotonous to him or how he just did not like anything at all about school. He would have given a thousand and one reasons for his disdain towards school.

But it was none of those things, perhaps it was just his nonchalant, careless attitude to learning and study that had coloured his view so badly and distorted it so much till he came to believe that school was not for people like him. This discolouration had sealed his disdain for school.

It would take years for him to come to that realisation, that he was the problem, not the school nor the teachers. But that chilly morning that he picked his way to school sandwiched by wet shrubs and long leafy grass on that lonely path, that was what he thought and believed; that learning and school was hard and not meant for people like him.

The first lesson for the day was English language. Oliver groaned, he did not like the English teacher, the truth was he did not like any of the teachers.

He was expecting the English teacher, Mr Harrison, a short, roundish man who placed emphasis on the correct pronunciation of words, but instead it was someone else that came. A young woman in her twenties, in a well ironed shirt and trousers and a face cap with the words N. Y. S. C. inscribed on it (National Youth Service Corps). She was a youth corper, and that meant she was mandated to serve the country for one year. Oliver figured she had been posted to serve as a teacher in his town's secondary school.

The young woman who called herself Josephine, smiled at them and told them she had a Bachelor of Arts in English and Literary studies and would be assisting Mr Harrison in teaching the class. She taught them with painstaking care and patience that first day, and at the end of the class, she informed them of an assignment.

She said she wanted them to get a book and document the new things, the new information, and the ideas that caught their attention whilst they listened to their teachers.

Corper Josephine told them it was a great way to learn and retain information, she told them that there was an ancient Chinese proverb that bore witness to what she told them. The Chinese believed, as expressed through the proverb, that the faintest ink is better than the strongest memory.

Oliver loved the proverb and the idea of the assignment. He committed himself to it and saw a great improvement in his academics.

Thus, this solidified the importance of writing in his heart. From experience, he learned that things were written down to ensure they were remembered and not discarded. He held the opinion that the only use of writing is documenting for remembrance. He believed this so much that he must have probably had a sign in his heart that reads, 'If you do not want to forget, write it down.'

However, years of growth, months of working out his goals, days after days of listening and learning from mentors, hours of reading great books and intentionally walking with his life's allies and distinguishers taught him that writing was more than a way of helping the memory.

One of his mentors explained to him that the act of recording each step of his journey was not just about memory; it was about deciphering the intricacies of his goals. So, the pen became his wand, and the parchment, a canvas waiting to capture the essence of his endeavours.

The pen was meant to unravel the details of his goals, it was not just to keep them from being forgotten. Oliver had called this mentor a week after his conversation with Maurice on how goals helped one to be observant, how it gave the goal setter keen eyes to recognize time and opportunities. The mentor was a lecturer from his days in the university. This man, Professor Clinton, took him like one of his sons. It was a timely unofficial adoption that happened when Oliver lost his father in his second year in the university. The news of his father's death plunged him into a sea of grief and despair that stuck like a stubborn stain on clothes to everything he did. He lost his zeal for life, his appetite dwindled, social interactions were kept to an unreasonable minimum, his average grades plummeted. He just did not see the reason for anything any more and justifiably so.

He came from poverty and saw how his mother and father struggled daily to give him and his siblings the best. They had been so committed to his growth that the only reason he felt a twinge of guilt for his non-sterling academic performance was for their sake. His academics did improve when he met Corper Josephine and when he secured admission into the university, he vowed to do his best, get good grades, get a good job and take care of his father and mother. He knew this was only possible if he was educated, for less privileged people like him, education is access to the seats of power. His father's death made a mockery of this vow. What was the point, he had asked himself, when the people you want to take care of are dying?

His grades kept going down, he was looking forward to the school advising him to withdraw, instead he got a call from his course advisor, Professor Clinton who was still an academic Doctor then.

He got to his office and the man smiled warmly at him and offered him a seat. He sat and Professor Clinton offered his condolences. Oliver was shocked into an upright seating position. He was dumbfounded. How did he know? He quizzed himself. Of course his class representatives and two of his classmates knew but that was it. No one else knew.

Professor Clinton answered his unasked question.

"Your class representative told me about your dad. Your grades are poor, and I wanted to know what was responsible for the sudden change since you were one of the best in class. I called him to ask about you, and he told me you lost your dad."

There was a brief pause, during which Professor Clinton stared gently and compassionately at him while he looked at everything but his course advisor

"Don't do this to yourself," Professor Clinton said after a few minutes.

That was all the cue Oliver needed to cry like a baby. He told the course advisor how he felt and at the end of that short but meaningful meeting, the adoption was sealed. Oliver had a new father, and Professor Clinton had a new son. He had since that time been an encouragement in Oliver's pursuit of purpose.

Daddy Clinton, as Oliver sometimes called him, listened to all he had to say during the phone conversation and told him his friend, Maurice, was on the right track, he however informed Oliver that to his observation he should include "Scripting".

"Scripting? What does that mean?" Oliver had asked, confused but expectant. This goal setting of a thing was taking on a life bigger than what he had envisaged, but he loved all of it. He was ready for everything it promised.

"My dear Oliver, success is scripted. It has to be scripted," the Professor said, and went on to teach him the intimate relationship between the pen and nurturing goals to maturity. He told him that his life is a book that had blank pages, recording his observations is the ink that would pen his success story in these pages.

He told him that life is a laboratory, it is like a scientist's work that demands meticulous record-keeping. Every twist and turn, every insight gained, and every hurdle crossed needs to be scripted in the narrative of his aspirations. Everything must be written, the challenges, the success, the fears, the triumphs. Nothing is too big or too small to document. All must be written, all must be given equal attention in this narrative that captures his sojourn to actualising his dreams.

Professor Clinton told Oliver that scripting is important because it is informative. Information holds power, and Oliver, by using his pen as a tool, can wield that power. What he documents would become the script of his success, a tangible representation of his aspirations. The recorded observations are not just notes; they are the keys to unlocking the doors of his goals. Reflecting on them becomes a journey back in time, a source of wisdom to navigate the uncertainties that lay ahead.

"Script your success, Oliver, script it." Professor Clinton concluded.

When the call ended, Oliver's heart burned with a renewed passion, fuelled by the knowledge that he just acquired. He was no longer going to leave his observations to the whirlwind of chance. He would no longer leave the lessons he had learnt undocumented and miss out on their potential for future endeavours.

He remembered the phone call and his resolution as he sat in his bed that evening after work. He realised he had not done what was needed, so he stood to his feet and walked to his writing table to start this process of scripting. He was ready to take another important step in the realisation of his dreams. As he walked towards the table, a statement from the Holy Book dropped into his heart.

It said, "From the fruit of his lips a man is filled with good things, as surely as the work of his hands rewards him." He understood the profoundness of the words and muttered a quick prayer of thanksgiving to God for giving him a word in season.

Oliver sat at his table, pulled the hard bound cover book closer and admired it. The exercise book of the earlier days of his goals setting had been replaced by something more durable and appealing. Oliver sometimes found it wondrous how setting your heart to a goal had the ability to change everything about a person. His thoughts, his perspectives, his decisions, the things he spends money on, the value he places on tools that would bring him closer to his vision, the importance he attached to those tools and how quickly he was able to do away with things that did not work. It also made him give special attention to the scrolls of those written desires, in this case the hard bound cover book he bought. The wonderful, transforming power of goals!

Oliver called himself back so he could concentrate on the task at hand: scripting his success. He flipped the cover and the pages of the book and began to write. As he wrote and marvelled at the ease with which he wrote, he realised that his journey was a narrative waiting to unfold. Each recorded observation was a waypoint, marking progress, pitfalls, and potential. The information he gathered was not to be cast aside; it was to be cherished as a compass for future reference. In the script of success, every word mattered.

He continued writing, happy at his findings and this new revelation. He wrote, already imagining the pitfalls he would successfully avoid because he took a decision to document his observations. He was happy about the acceleration his goals would gain because he realised early that information is power, most especially information that he recorded; because the information is from him, lived by him, and from his own observation.

Oliver continued writing. He wrote purposefully, as fast as someone with a grudge to settle.

When he was done writing, he flipped through the pages of the notes and sought guidance from his own narrative. The words he had penned became a guiding light in the darkness of uncertainty. The script of success was not just about achievements; it was about the lessons learned, the challenges overcome, and the growth experienced.

Oliver was happy with his work, but at the same time he reminded himself to be sober. This scripting of success should not be a one time thing. He decided to write the reason in his book. He wrote:

*Recording observations is not just a task but a practice—a habit that shapes one's perspective. The pen becomes a companion, and the act of scripting success , a deliberate effort to carve one's path in the grand tapestry of life.*

This is a good thing to note, Oliver thought as he continued writing what he felt about the notion of scripting one's way to success.

He further wrote that,

"Observation and record-keeping are powerful Siamese twins in goal actualisation. They should be done together."

The script of success is an ongoing process, and with each chapter, he adds new pages to the story of his aspirations. The laboratory of life, with its experiments and discoveries, would become the canvas on which he would paint the masterpiece of his success. When Oliver finished writing, he laughed and threw his hands up in the air.

"Yes! This is it!"

"Thank God," he said with a heart full of gratitude.

# NAVIGATING THE SEAS OF KNOWLEDGE

There was a centre of attraction close to the house Oliver lived in, he had rented the flat three months into his job as a factory worker. This centre attracted all manner of people. It often had an unusual attention drawn to it in the mornings. People make a dash for it as ants run to sugar, even those that had a place to go in the mornings usually spared it a quick glance as they hurried off to their offices and places of business. The ones with time to spare crowded around its offerings, pushing and jostling against one another for space. They often quarrel, and a lot had left the place with grudges they did not come with. The place had a powerful hold that people made references to it in conversations, they even look forward to the bantering and gave it as a descriptive landmark to people who had a reason to come to the street.

Ironically, this centre of attraction had nothing in terms of beauty or grandeur to warrant such attention. It was a stall held together by measly, termite infested logs of wood, its roof was made with rusty roofing sheets that had obviously seen better days. This stall stood pathetically over a sandy ground. On its floor was a long and wide, sturdy wooden table. The table was the only durable thing in this stall that attracted so-much-often-wondered-about people. The table was manned by a middle-aged man whose shirt somehow always managed to sparkle and stay unruffled amidst the rancour the stall witnessed on a daily basis.

The stall had just one offering; newspapers. The stall was a newspaper stand and the man that manned it was the newspaper vendor. The maniac rush of people to this stall most mornings was a testament to how drawn humans were to information, how readily they soaked it up, and how interested they were in gathering facts and learning new things.

Not even money or the lack of it stopped people in this impoverished street from going to the newspaper stands. Some bought, while most stood around the table, gleaning what they could from the headlines boldly written on the front pages.

A fool says information is nothing, but the wise man knows that information is power. Oliver knew he needed quality information if he was going to navigate the seasons of his life well. He thought of this as he walked past the newspaper stall that was characteristically filled with people.

"Brother Oliver, good morning." Someone called. Oliver turned and waved at the caller with a smile.

It was his neighbour's ten years old son. The boy helped him with errands and had always refused his 'thank you' money, so he made a mental note to get him a befitting and useful gift soon. A book, perhaps.

The thought of a book called his mind to his initial thought before the boy's call, so he continued to think of information as he walked to the bus stop. Information is power, and it is one power no genuine goal-setter and purpose chaser should take lightly.

In the vast expanse of dreams, Oliver has come to realise that information was the compass guiding his ship through the uncharted waters of success. It wasn't merely about aiming; it was about hitting the target with precision. Every dreamer, he thought, needed to equip themselves with the right principles and gather the necessary information to craft their success.

Every warrior with an intention to win a war never goes to the war front empty-handed, he goes fully armed.

Such should be the life of a goal setter, to ensure good success in his endeavours, he must be fully armed and equipped with information. It helps to forestall the goal setter beating around the uncharted bush of his purpose aimlessly.

Oliver got to the bus stop and flagged down a bike.

"Harcourt bookstore," he told the rider

"The one behind the community bank?" The rider asked.

"Yes, that one." Oliver responded.

The rider told him the fare and Oliver took the seat behind him. As the bike sped down the tarred road, Oliver's heart warmed at the prospect of spending his Saturday off work at a bookstore, glancing through the pages of books written by people who had gone ahead and left their experiences, challenges, and failures as a learning pad so that he could read and avoid their mistakes, learn from their resilience, and be encouraged by their success. It was a luxury his job as a barrow pusher could never afford him. The factory job was nowhere near what he aimed for, but he was grateful.

Gratitude is one virtue he believes every dreamer should have in abundance. It makes the process and journey of becoming a success tolerable and less overwhelming.

When Oliver got to the bookstore, he took one enthusiastic step after the other around the tables laden with books. He walked in between the shelves heavy with books, smiling like a child who was given a treat.

When a sales attendant walked up to him and asked if he needed help, he smiled and said, "No, thank you ma'am, I am a regular here I can find my way around."

When she left, Oliver picked a book from the shelf and ran through the pages, checking to see if the thoughts of the author were good enough to earn his hard-earned cash. However, as he flipped through, page after page, the voice of Professor Clinton echoed strongly through his mind, demanding his urgent attention.

Professor Clinton once told him that the principles of success were not just in books, it was in the people who had walked the path before him. Professor Clinton also said that the people who surrounded him would ultimately become the pavement on his path—some assisting, some hindering, and some attempting to extinguish his flame. Oliver took this lesson to heart: choosing companions wisely was like selecting keys to the vault of information.

Information was not just in books, it was also in people, so he had to be careful who he allowed to have access to his life. People were not only life carriers, they were also information bearers and a tardy decision in carefully choosing friends, companions, and mentors could have destructive effects on his goals.

His mentor and adopted father clarified this by making certain distinctions. He said some people were distinguishers while the others were extinguishers.

The distinguishers are the beacons that propel him toward his dreams. These are the mentors, the guides, the ones that understand the value of comprehensive information. While the extinguishers are those who could dim his flame and so should have no access to his future. The journey to his dreams, Professor Clinton had enthused, required not just ambition but also discernment.

It is imperative that Oliver become as gentle as a dove and as wise as a serpent. He has to be discerning. There is a need for him to filter everything that comes to him, the information and the people. It is a necessary step towards his glorious future.

Oliver saw a book that he liked, so he picked it. He saw another one and picked it too. At the third pick, he asked himself if he really knew the importance of information. If he really knew why it was critical to success, if he really knew what he should do with the knowledge and information he was going to acquire from the books he was buying.

Was information and knowledge an end in itself, or a means to an end? He knew the right answer because he once had a conversation about it with Maurice the first time he came to this bookstore.

He had been so impressed at Maurice's purchase that he had hailed him as a bookworm. His friend had smiled in his calm and unassuming way and told him the gospel truth that he would never forget. Maurice told him that his journey was not just about accumulating knowledge; it was about strategically understanding how to apply that knowledge.

It is knowledge acquired and applied that makes a man successful. Knowledge acquired and left to waste bodes no good to the acquirer. The only thing such acquisition does is to puff up and give a grandiose sense of importance that profit no one, the acquirer especially.

Maurice continued by saying that in the navigation of the seas of knowledge, each wave carrying him must bring him closer to his aspirations. He told Oliver that he recently realised that comprehensive information wasn't just about facts; it was about knowing how to use those facts strategically, and this is the key to unlocking doors and overcoming obstacles.

Oliver treasured Maurice's words and kept them securely in his heart, he put them into practice and subsequently found that as he moved further in his journey, he understood that information was not stagnant; it was dynamic. What worked yesterday might not work tomorrow. Thus, the quest for knowledge is a continuous endeavour.

There is no end to learning. There is no end to

getting valuable information, and there is no end to putting what has been learnt into action. The goal-setter must be ready to become a lifelong student. The distinguishers in his life: the mentors who share their experiences will become living textbooks guiding him through the evolving landscape of success.

Understanding principles, seeking guidance, and letting wisdom be a compass became Oliver's mantra. As he gathered information, he was also mindful of the invaluable role that time and chance played in everyone's life.

Thus, confidently, Oliver's ship sailed with purpose and direction. The compass of information guided him through storms of uncertainty and calm seas of opportunity. The distinguishers, the principles, and the wisdom acquired through comprehensive information became the wind in his sails, propelling him toward the horizon of success.

# A BLANK CANVAS

In the quaint town where he grew up, Oliver's family's name was not worth much. They were a secured member of the dregs of their community. His family was not wealthy, and opportunities seemed scarce. He grew up seeing his parents struggle day in and day out for the basic needs of life. His father did undignified but legal jobs that sometimes made him come home to cry behind closed doors. On countless occasions, Oliver had overheard him tell his mother about the insults he got at work. Yet he kept pushing, he kept showing up, he kept going back to work until the day he collapsed under the weight of it. His mother was no different, she sold petty household goods in the market, and to fast track sales she often pushed wheelbarrows around the market and streets where her customers lived. Oliver had many times gone on this marketing adventure with her, it was a task he hated. If only he had caught a glimpse of the future, to see how the job that he loathed would later be the channel through which he would get his first real job after graduation.

"Do not despise the days of little beginnings," was a popular statement in the town Oliver grew up in. It was a frequent feature in religious gatherings and circles. A simple, yet meaningful statement. Oliver often wondered if the people he knew who reiterated these words actually knew what it meant. Their endeavours showed that while their mouths said the words, their attitude and perspective had not been conformed to the reality of those words. He knew this because he saw them, he saw the fruits their labours bore. Oliver was lucky because he reasoned differently. Just like the two Israelites spies sent to the promised land gave Moses a different faith-filled report, Oliver also had a different report.

Whenever he thinks of this, he remembers the role his parents played in re-engineering his mind.

Oliver's parents were dealt a hard hand by life, but they were not willing to settle. Their hearts burned with a passion for more, a passion for a change of status, a desire for an elevation. It was a desire that was further strengthened when a guest minister to their church had encouraged parents to help their children create a reading culture. He asserted the need for this by telling the gathered congregants the story of Ben Carson and how books changed his life. This added more fuel to the already burning passion in Oliver's father's heart, and he transferred the same to him. Thus, Oliver was equally fuelled by a passion for achieving his dreams, no matter their size. Books became his friends and the town's library, one of his favourite hideaways. Since he could not afford to buy books, he spent most of his free days in the library.

Amidst the challenge of limited resources, Oliver stumbled upon an old book at the town's library. Chapter Five of the book was titled 'Start Small: The Only Joy in the World is to Begin.' The words resonated deeply within him as he read about the power of seizing even the smallest opportunities.

These words glowed in his heart, so much that he could not stop talking about it. He told them to his father one day, and he patted his back and smiled at him. He told him to hold fast to those words, because he'll need them one day.

And the day did come.

After a year and six months in the factory where he

worked, the strings of his heart began to play the tunes of his ancestral home. His attention was pulled to things he had before that time not given much thought to. There arose in his heart a yearning that only the journey to his hometown could quench.

He began to notice opportunities around the town that he had previously overlooked. The local market presented a chance for him to start a small venture. Oliver came to the realisation that he could start by using what he already had in order to fulfil his dream of improving his community.

The stories he had read from books in the library and the ones he was feeding on pointed that his quest was good. They gave him a template and assurance of success in this untrodden path he intended to embark on.

So Oliver committed his desires to God in prayers and called the distinguishers in his life.  A wise man once said that in the multitudes of counsellors there is safety. Oliver knew his goals and desires were safe in their hands because they were not extinguishers who would quench his fire.

Professor Clinton applauded his venture and gave his blessings. Maurice shed a few tears, told him he would miss him, bought him books on how to successfully run a small business, and gave his blessings. He resigned from the factory and set sail for his hometown to start his new business.

Oliver rented a modest kiosk with the little money he had saved, he felt a mix of fear and excitement. The journey was uncertain, but he took the first step. Every day, he opened his kiosk, and as he worked around it, imagined what his business could be. He thought of the day his small kiosk would evolve into a thriving venture, exceeding his initial expectations.

He imagined his business would be so successful that tongues would begin to wag. And while others made speculations about his success, those who would ask questions, wondering how he did it and in such a short time too would be given answers. To those that chose rumour mongering, he would leave them to their devices and choose to remain focused. He would open his arms to those who are genuinely surprised at his success and wanted to learn how he did it so they can replicate such success in a town that everyone had given up all hope on. Out of the abundance of his heart, and of the wisdom he had gained learning from others, from mentors and like-minded purpose driven companions, he would give freely.

With these new mentees and learners, he would not mince words, he would tell them about the necessity of setting smart goals, how important their goals are to their lives and how it should not be handled with levity. He would tell them about the keen observing eyes that goals give to goal setters and the need to cherish information and document processes. He would also tell them the wisdom of putting the knowledge acquired to practice and teach them how he had been able to make a success of his small business.

Oliver sat in his kiosk and continued to dream as he awaited customers. He saw his kiosk, but it was no longer small, it was a huge and beautiful building. He saw people coming in and going out with smiles from satisfied services. He saw protegees seated around his table listening and learning from his wealth of wisdom.

He saw himself expounding these mysteries to them. He imagined that he would tell them that behind his glorious business success, the attention he was getting and the seemingly unending sales, were months of tears and doubts and fears. He would tell them that he encountered setbacks and doubts, but the teachings from the books he had read, and a book he read many years ago in the town's library particularly, fuelled his determination to start small. He would tell them one of the stories from the book, the story of a man who started a successful business with a fraction of the expected capital. The lesson was clear: don't wait for the perfect conditions; start with what you have.

He would tell them he learnt from that man and

replicated the same in his life, bringing to bear the principle of applying knowledge. He not only acknowledged, he put the knowledge he got into use. Like that successful businessman he read about, he did not wait for when the situations were perfect, nor when he had all he needed, he started with what he had. He imagined instructing them that even the Holy Books lend credence to the sentiments espoused in the stories he told them.

The wise man once said in his book that, "Whoever watches the wind will not plant; whoever looks at the clouds will not reap."

He would instruct them not to wait for the perfect situation to start, and his success is evidence that starting small does not mean staying small. His success showed that one can become big from a small place. The beginning is the most crucial part of any endeavour, and thus should not be taken lightly.

It was akin to one of his mentor's favourite saying; "Better is a little with the fear of the Lord than greater treasure with trouble." Because of this, his fears about starting small, were doused to an almost insignificant fraction. It was from this same mentor that he heard about B. C. Forbes, from whom he learnt not to aim without acting. He also internalised the idea that the man who is afraid to begin is worse than a quitter.

He proposed in his heart that he would not have his

future students ignorant, he would tell them his journey was proof that success is not an overnight occurrence; it is a gradual process that rewards those who dare to start.

However, while starting small was good, there is need for an internal configuration that is needed to help them stay committed to what they have started. That internal configuration is called 'Persistence'.

The only joy in the world is not just in beginning or creating; it is in the tenacity to continue, to keep painting even when faced with challenges. Every stroke requires effort; every detail demands perseverance. As the canvas absorbed layers of dedication, he would tell them that he came to the understanding that the journey was not a sprint but a marathon. And that, through the rhythm of persistence, the masterpiece of his life would take shape. The colours would blend seamlessly, forming a narrative of resilience and determination. The only joy in the world, he knew, was in the journey itself, in the process of becoming, and in the unwavering belief that every stroke brought him closer to the fulfilment of his dreams.

His dexterity was as a result of years of sacrifices, learning, sleepless nights, counsels from mentors and working out his goals. It was a dexterity that was cultivated and not stumbled upon.

Oliver made a solemn promise to share all he had

learnt.

A customer's voice from the next store woke Oliver up. He stirred himself from his daydream and said a quick prayer. He prayed that his dream would come to pass. That he would be known as a success and not just a dreamer. He prayed that through his success, others in the town would also be emboldened to seek theirs.

He prayed just as he had dreamt that his story would inspire others to overcome their hesitations and begin their journeys, no matter how small the first step might be. The joy lay in the steady rhythm of persistence, in the unwavering commitment to see his creation through to its completion. And he prayed that one day the blank canvas would be a testament to his endurance.

# CONQUERING SHADOWS

Not many in the town of Evergreen told the story of Kennedy. They knew the story of Benedict, the painter, but the stories about Kennedy and what became of him were as scant as the wealth that eluded the town for years. There was a hush and shroud of secrecy around it, like most cautionary tales.

It was a story that parents used as a last resort, but when Oliver heard it, he wondered about it. Kennedy's story was all the motivation a visionary needed to pull up his boots straps and do right by his dreams.

Oliver heard it for the first time from his mother. It was weeks after his return to the town. The rent for his kiosk had been paid, and the repairs had been done. His goods had been bought and were wrapped neatly in cartons in his old room. He should have been in his kiosk, arranging his goods on the shelves and calling out to customers, instead he was staring at the cracked and unpainted walls of his room and thinking away in the morning.

All the surge of emotions and motivation that had hastened his resignation and his trip back to the town had suddenly waned off.

Week in week out he stared at his goods, he thought of the kiosk waiting for his presence and doubted his decision. What was he thinking? What got into him? How could he possibly think it was possible? The initial euphoria of starting a business was gone. Nothing prospered in the town! The high rate of failures in lives and businesses in the town stood in contrast against the name of the town; Evergreen. Things did not go green, they died, they withered. People left to prosper, what level of delusion made him believe his story would be different? He should have just stayed in the factory he left and worked his way up.

This became his daily routine. Wake up. Bathe. Eat. Stare at his goods. Bemoan his fate. Shed hidden tears of regret. Sleep. All this while the rest of the world got busy and chased their dreams.

His dreams had been hit on the legs by fear and he did not even know it.

Thank goodness for his mother.

She came in that day and called his name fondly.

He smiled in response.

She sat beside him and held his hands

"What is the problem, my son?"

Oliver knew better than to evade the question or pretend all was fine. His mother read him like a familiar book.

"This, this business, thi..this ..thing," he stammered.

"Yes," his mother said, staring intently at him and encouraging him to talk.

"This business, my coming back to this town, I don't know if it was the right thing."

"Do you feel right about it here?" His mother asked, as she tapped her hand on his chest.

Oliver sighed and stood to his feet, towering over his mother.

"I don't know, I guess I am just scared," he said softly, his voice carrying all the emotions he felt. It was a confession he never knew he would one day make about himself. He thought he had gone past it. He thought he had read enough books and learnt enough from mentors to fall into that trap again. But there he was, confessing it to his mother, and hoping for the best.

"I will tell you a story," his mother said. Oliver rolled his eyes and laughed.

His mother adjusted herself on the chair as she told the story.

Kennedy was the town's comedian, but for every funny joke, there were hundreds of crude and unnecessary ones. Jokes that rub off irritatingly on people's sensibilities. It was clear to the discerning that the jokes were a mask for something deep, a hurt that time had failed to heal. He toured the town most days looking for free food and doing odd jobs. In his drunken stupor, he competed with the birds in serenading the town to sleep at night. With no family, no life, not even a farm to his name, Kennedy had little to be admired for.

But he had not always been like that.

There was a time Kennedy was driven, resourceful, and ambitious. There was a time his goals had kept him up at night, and when he slept his dreams had been filled with solutions and possibilities. Like most visionaries, he had put his hands where his mouth was. He embarked on a series of ventures that held promises of prosperity for the town and for him.

He secured a contract to be a major distributor for a product from Evergreen but chickened out. His fears got the best part of him. The company took their products to a neighbouring town and the prosperity it brought to that town and their distributor there was all the answers Kennedy needed to know that he was wrong to not see the deal through.

A decision with the imprint of fear.

He did not try again or fight for his dreams. He just sank into depression and became the town's jester. A man who made jokes out of everything he once held dear.

After the story, Oliver's mother stood and held his gaze. She wagged a finger in his face and said, "Don't become another Kennedy."

When she left, Oliver picked up a carton of his goods and made for the door. Kennedy's story was all the motivation he needed. He would no longer be bound by fear.

Coincidentally, the chapter of the book he was reading was about fear. Fear, the silent adversary lurking in the shadows, ready to cripple dreams and shatter aspirations. Fear, the killer of dreams, the subtle assassin that whisper doubts into the hearts of dreamers.

Many dreams have died prematurely because of fear. And where the dreams did not die, fear had spoken doubts over and over again until the dreams had lost potency.

As he read, Oliver saw fear as an arrow wielded by the enemy to destroy the dreams, goals, and aims of goal-getters like him. He reckoned that the ability to reject the evil thought of fear, to say to oneself, 'Not so,' marks the first step towards victory.

Oliver stopped reading and pondered on those words 'Not so,' he wished Kennedy had said that. He wished he had set his face like a flint and had screamed 'NOT SO!' to the destructive voice of fear. He wished he had sought counsel from a courageous person who would have helped dispel his doubts. Oliver knew Kennedy's story would have been his story but for the timely counsel of his mother. How he wished Kennedy got the same. He closed his eyes and, for the umpteenth time, thanked God for the gift of mentors and counsellors. They surrounded him as a shield and have helped him wage war against the adversaries of his future, adversaries like fear.

An adversary that had rendered the dreams of men useless and made the dreamers less of the men they ought to be. Fear had taken the wind from their sail and made them settle for the crumbs that fell from tables when their seat should have been at the table. Stories abound of men and women whose lives took an unplanned pause because they chose to listen to the whispers of fear. Their dreams were paralysed by the power of fear. There were those who, at the first hint of adversity, abandoned their dreams for the comfort of the familiar.

There were also those whose passions became cold and forgotten because of their fear of people and people's opinions. They cherished their image in the hearts of men more than the image of greatness in their own hearts. An extremely great and unnecessary price to pay for the unstable opinions of people.

As Oliver flipped through the pages, he learnt that men could also be agents of fear. These men, through their words and actions, instil fear in the hearts of the dreamer. They give reports that discourage courageous decisions. The truth is, no one can rise above the mental fortitude, emotional strength and attitudes of the people that surround him.

Therefore, to overcome fear, the dreamer must acknowledge certain truths;

The first is that fear would never go away. It may reduce to an almost unrecognisable size, but it would never not be a part of a human emotion. It will rear its head at odd times, like when a thing is done for the first time, or when a regular thing is done before a new audience or virgin circumstances. The doubt it whispers may never disappear, but it can lose its potency. The wise dreamer is the one that takes the necessary steps in spite of the suggestions made by fear. So, when the book said overcoming fear requires a deliberate decision to take every concern and every decision into cognizance, Oliver agreed.

Secondly, the dreamer must take deliberate actions

to filter his circle of friends and associates, else his dreams are undermined by people whose language is fear. He has to make a decision to do what ought to be done, irrespective of how his fear makes him feel. He has to learn that doing it afraid is better than not making an effort.

Fear, Oliver also realised, is not a roadblock but an opportunity for success. This is a truth that discerning and successful men have discovered. Often times, what laid on the flip side of fear was not more fear or failure, what laid there was success. Growth and self awareness lay on the other side of fear. When a man faces obstacles headlong, instead of cowering in fear, he not only learns strategies on how to face other obstacles, he gains a deeper sense of who he is, his abilities, and what these abilities can do for him. Nothing is as powerful as a self-aware man who has conquered fear.

The chapter also told the tale of Joseph and the founder of Kentucky Fried Chicken, it emphasised that a setback could be a set-up for success. Fear and failure were not barriers but stepping stones toward greatness.

With each word, Oliver felt a surge of courage, a determination to reject fear and embrace faith. The last paragraph echoed with a resounding truth—fear could stop you from attaining maximum success. He took the charge to heart, realising that like other great and successful men before him, nothing could stop him when he believes that there are no limitations and lives unafraid.

Armed with a newfound courage, Oliver closed the book, he knew the journey ahead was challenging, but he would walk with the assurance that fear was no longer his master, and the dreams that danced in his heart were within reach.

# THE SYMPHONY OF FAITH

Oliver garnered students long before his business became a household name. His dream of impacting lives was coming true, but sometimes he wondered what they saw, his store was still small and his sales erratic. But he also acquiesced that maybe all a person needs to affix himself to another as a student went beyond the scope of material things. People seek for courageous and fearless people. They live in awe of risk-takers. They are enamoured with men and women of principles and when they see people who fit these descriptions, they pitch their tents in spite of the supposed wealth or lack of it of the tutor or mentor.

Oliver had some of those. He had students and they came to learn. They found him worthy of listening to.

These optimistic visionaries believed he had an answer to the questions that plagued their heart. They believed his counsel could make beauty out of their mess. He was the one that had trod the path they never knew existed, showing them that there was inherent beauty and wealth in their land. He came to build a successful business in a land that people were deserting, showing them that all their fertile land needed was their fertile minds to flourish. Telling that the fertility of mind is a product of knowledge, resilience, right attitude, and a large dose of faith.

They had come to learn because they knew he would give freely from his wealth of knowledge, as he had been doing. Through one man, ideas would be brought to life, businesses would be birthed, and the town would have a new lease of life. Oliver had done what no man had done before in the town. He was, to the town, more than a hundred sons. He had stayed resolute in spite of prevailing challenges. He had left a job in the city to start a business in a town people could not wait to leave. And every time he opened his kiosk, it showed them the triumph of his faith over his fears. He was a man worth learning from.

The word spread fast.

There was a guru in town.

"Guru." Oliver scoffed at the word as he took his seat

and faced his students, the same way he scoffed the first time he heard the title.

He was no guru, just a man of great faith, a faith that had fought fear. An ordinary man like them whose fears would have won if he was not helped to see beyond his circumstances and believe that the future he saw was possible. The future he is still working towards.

He is not a guru, he is just a normal everyday man who chose faith over fear daily. He is far from being a guru, and he hoped his session with his students would attest to that.

He used the book he was reading as a tool and read a chapter to his audience. He started with the title

"Apply faith."

"Apply faith," he said again, this time slowly, gently, hoping the word will resonate with his audience.

"I said apply faith!" A declaration and command that he prayed his audience would take to heart.

"What is faith?" someone from the audience asked.

Oliver smiled and continued reading from the book.

"Faith," he said, "is a force that bridges the gap between the seen and the unseen, the tangible and the intangible."

Faith is what brings into tangibility what formerly existed as figments of imagination. It is what brings into reality, the visions of a future. The unseen becomes seen when faith is mixed with it.

A wise author once defined faith as the assurance of things hoped for and the conviction of things not seen.

"So, to succeed in life, all we need is faith in God?" another student asked.

"Faith in God and faith in yourself," Oliver answered.

In the course of his journey, Oliver had come to realise that faith, as a tool for success, is a two-headed sword that needed to be deployed with wisdom. Some who failed to take advantage of this delicate balance, have made a wreck of their journey.

Faith in God is a necessity, but faith in oneself is also to be esteemed.

The successful person believes in God's ability and also believes in himself. He recognises that in him are treasures and wisdom untold for the ills and problems of his world. His responsibility is to discover and see these treasures for what they are; solutions. And when seen, to believe that it has the ability to change his life and his world when put into use. He has to believe that his gifts, no matter how crude it looks, have the power to create a desirable future for him.

Oliver felt a surge of courage, and he declared to his students boldly that they must have faith in God and faith in themselves if they want to achieve great feats.

"Do you understand this?" he asked.

They nodded in response.

"Have you ever tried cutting a tree with a blunt axe?"

"You know how strenuous that can be, right?" he continued without waiting for a response.

"Now equate the blunt axe to doubt. Doubt is the tool that will never give you what you want, no matter how hard you try. Faith on the other hand is to a tree what a sharp axe is, just a few precise and strategic cuts and the tree is down."

"Wow," someone said. Oliver smiled.

"You get the picture? So faith is the axe that breaks the yoke of impossibility, fear, and uncertainty."

Oliver told them to imagine a mighty axe, swinging through the barriers of doubt, clearing a path towards their dreams and aspirations. Faith informs the dreamer that the dream is possible.

It is through faith that problems are surmounted. It is faith that ensures visions are held on to when troubles besiege it. Faith in what is unseen that the dreamer knows is possible, keeps the embers burning. It stokes the fire of passion in the heart of the dreamer, else it dies.

Faith is the secret of men who triumphed over life's adversities and stamped their names in history. Faith and doubt are the defining factor in the lives of those who became and those whom nothing came from.

To goals, knowledge, diligence, and the staying power of faith must be added. It is faith that creates possibilities out of uncertainties.

Oliver closed the book and told them the story of a master builder.

Just like him, this master builder left certainty for uncertainty. He left luxury for purpose. He went by the name, Nehemiah, and he carried in his heart a love for his nation that made complacency impossible. It was a love that called him into building. He built walls that kept the enemies at bay and secured his people.

Nehemiah had a vision to build, but it was a vision that was tested. However, like all men of faith, Nehemiah refused to give up. He did not dim the light of his dream. He allowed his faith to give wings to his passion. His vision to rebuild did not die in the face of trials. He chose resilience in the face of failure, and the unwavering belief that there would always be a way out of every dilemma—a decision fuelled by faith, made him an overcomer. Oliver saw Nehemiah as a beacon of inspiration, a testament to the power of faith in overcoming challenges.

He also narrated to them stories of visionaries and dreamers who, armed with faith, lived in a separate world—a world where defeat was but a fleeting illusion.

Men like Benedict, the town's famous painter and artist. Not many people knew that behind the success that was seen and so glamorously celebrated were years of denials and rejections. After his stint at the university, all attempts to show his works at exhibitions were rejected. He needed his arts to be in people's faces, but for years it only went past the faces of those who commissioned him to work for them. Those were the long, arduous days that would have made a less resolved man to turn back and ditch his dreams, but not Benedict. Benedict was made from a stronger stock. He had a dream that not even the hardest of times could dissuade from coming into reality. His faith brought him into the clan of achievers. His faith gave him a seat with men who through sheer grit, belief in God and their abilities dominated spheres. Men who have made a vow with unending success via their faith.

"Any assessment of Benedict's success that tries to explain away his unwavering faith as being pivotal to his success is false," Oliver told them.

"Faith," he told them, "is the organic acid that dissolves the spirit of impossibilities in one's goals. It is the force that moves God to act, the key that brings the enemy to one's command."

The whole world stands still for the man who dares to believe. For the man of faith, God will move a thousand mountains. In a crowd of millions, God's hands will locate the man who dares to believe. Faith attracts, and when a man believes, he sets himself up for goodness untold. Such is the power of faith.

As the words unfolded, Oliver felt a profound sense of responsibility—to believe in the unfailing power of God, to release his faith until his goals were achieved. It was a desire he hoped to replicate in his students. He would raise men who believe in God and in the abilities He had put in them. Men who through faith would mount up as eagles on the mountains of life.

"However, you should know this; faith is active." Oliver said.

Faith is not passive, it is active and alive and a propeller of corresponding actions. What is believed about the future must find expression through action. Faith without work is useless.

It is the sum total of these daily faith filled actions that brings about the expected future, and sometimes these actions will come decked in the garb of risk.

Anyone who dares to believe in the impossible, must be ready to take actions, even ones that outrightly borders on risk. Oliver contemplated the words of Richard Divos and told them. He said, "The only thing that stands between a man and what he wants from life is often merely the will to try it and the faith to believe that it is possible."

The thought lingered in the air, Oliver looked at his students, one face to the other. He was happy the words had the desired effect. He wanted them to embrace the will to try and the faith to believe.

He reminded them of his story, of the risk he took in coming back to a town that almost everyone had written off. He told them of the job he left, yes it was a job beneath his qualifications but just like his friend, Maurice, he had been on his way up the company's administrative ladder with one promotion in the bag. He left that certainty for a life in a town where the lifespan for businesses like his was six months. There was a great future ahead if he succeeded, but the chances of success were slim. But, fuelled by faith in God and in his abilities, he took the risk that he believed would make a success out of him.

"No, no, no," Oliver said with a wave of the hand when his students clapped.

"I do not need the applause, I said all that to let you know that your faith must always lead you to take actions. What if the actions are risky? So be it, man up and face the challenge, you have everything you need to overcome."

Oliver concluded his address with a powerful truth, "Only those who risk going too far can possibly find out how far one can go."

The symphony of faith played on, and when Oliver closed the book, the echoes of courage and conviction lingered in his heart. There was a sudden burst of energy and faith to do more, to do the impossible and take on more challenges. He prayed that his students would feel the same.

The path ahead was uncertain, but faith illuminated the way, daring him to step into the unknown and discover the extraordinary within the ordinary.

# EMBERS OF DILIGENCE

Oliver learnt early in life that when you want something, you put in the work and do it well. The application of this knowledge had done him well in his business. He did all that was needed to do to ensure his business became successful. He left no stone unturned. If business was what he committed his heart to do, then he was duty bound to do it well. He would not waste his time on the bed when he should be in his kiosk selling. He would not engage in unproductive conversations when he should be tidying his account. He would not choose fruitless activities when he should be thinking of innovative ways to scale his business. He learnt this as a teenager.

He was fourteen and all the trappings of teenage hood were in full bloom. It came out in outbursts of angst at any and everything. There were occasional run-ins with his parents. There was a search for answers to questions that childhood shielded him from. Who am I? What am I doing here? What will I become? Questions that added to the confusion that puberty was known for.

His body was growing beyond his recognition, and there was a warmness in his heart whenever he saw a member of the opposite sex that he liked. Added to all these changes was peer pressure and Timberland boots.

When puberty came, Oliver found his own cool group, they were just a group of teenage boys with nothing in common but their broken voices, their shared confusion, their unfounded anger at authority figures, and their love for Timberland boots.

Timberland boots were the in thing then, everyone had one, or so it seemed to Oliver because he was the only one in his cool group without one. So yes, everyone in the whole world had Timberland boots except Oliver. Exaggeration much? But what was a little hyperbole to a teenager who wanted to feel included.

Talking to his parents about it was out of it. He knew they could not afford it. But when he saw a friend who like him came from an impoverished home with the revered and cherished Timberland boots, a surprised

Oliver walked up to him and asked him how he got it.

"My parents bought it," was his answer.

"Wow," Oliver said, masking his shock with a smile.

His mind worked fast, it told him, "Oliver, if his parents can buy it for him, yours should be able to buy yours too."

Who knows, his parents might have money stacked somewhere, and maybe they would not mind spending a bit of it on their loving, dutiful boy. Aside from recent squabbles and arguments, he had been a good son. He had helped his mother push barrows in the market and in the town's street. He had helped his father with many odd jobs, helped him deliver his farm produce to customers, and his grades had improved. Besides, he rarely asks for things like that. They should be able to give him some money.

So, he asked his father one night after dinner while he was resting under the big tree in their compound, slouched in the cane chair, picking his teeth with a broomstick.

His father had looked at him as if a nut had gone loose in his head, and with that same bewildered expression had asked him how much this Timberland boot was. When Oliver told him the price, his father laughed so hard he coughed.

After he drank the cup of water that Oliver brought,

he looked at him and told him with a tone of finality that he did not have that kind of money. Oliver knew better than to give reasons or explain. He knew how the family dynamics worked.

"Thank you," he said as he dragged his feet back to the room he shared with his siblings.

"Oliver!" his father called him to come closer. When he did, his father asked if he wanted the shoe.

"Boots," Oliver wanted to correct but kept quiet. What was the difference anyway, he thought, he was not getting either of the two.

"Yes sir," he replied.

"Then work for it, go and find something to do and work for it."

Oliver was not expecting that part of the conversation, and it left him at a loss for a suitable response, so he just nodded his head and left.

After days of seething over his father's proposition– what kind of father asks his son to go look for a job for something as paltry as boots– and bemoaning his fate, he heeded.

He wanted the Timberland boots to roll with his clique of wearers, so he got a job.

It was with a carpenter. One of the busiest in the town. His job requirement was to keep the carpenter's shed clean and run errands. He did his job well, and for his efficiency his pay was increased. In three months, his Timberland boots were bought. It was a purchase that needed six months of his wages. But his attitude to work and diligence cut the journey into half.

It was in this uncanny, unexpected way, with a job he had been reluctant to take, that Oliver learnt his first lesson in diligence: doing a job or work well was what made the difference and not just doing the job.

So, when chapter ten of the book he was reading says, "Be Hard-Working: Whatever Is Worth Doing at All Is Worth Doing Well." Oliver dived in because it was a turf he was familiar with. It's funny how the book seems to mirror his life and experiences.

As Oliver navigated the narrative, he continued to marvel at how the book drew parallels between the teachings and his own life. Diligence does not end with doing a job, instead it is in doing that job so well that excellence is produced. It is a conscientious decision to do well and to the very best of your abilities, any work committed into your hands. It is the ability to deploy all the resources within your reach and your means to the work in your hands. With diligence, the meagreness of the work to be done should never be a factor. The same level of attention, of expertise and devotion must be given to every type, size, and level of work. There should be no dichotomy. Great things should be done greatly.

Small things should be done excellently. That is the hallmark of greatness. It is the insignia of great men.

The chapter touched on the essence of humility, and Oliver agreed with the author. It takes a certain kind of lowliness of heart, of humility to do one's job well, even if the job was below one's perceived status and abilities. A diligent man is a humble man. The diligent man is a humble and purposeful man that embraces any task given to him, no matter how lowly it is. It is men like this that ascend to their desired level. Diligence has a price, but it also has a prize. Oliver saw himself in that narrative, ready to tackle every challenge with humility and perseverance and old-fashioned diligence.

With wide-eyed curiosity, Oliver continued reading the chapter, finding himself captivated by the words that unfolded before him. The chapter urged him to tread the highway of the upright and forsake the thorny path of laziness. Diligence is the antidote to laziness. Diligence, old, time trusted hard work is a type of wisdom.

And this wisdom of hard work, like a guiding star, illuminated Oliver's thoughts. He pondered the words of Myles Munroe and concluded that potential was not just a distant concept, but a dormant force waiting to be unleashed.

It is a force that listens only to the tune of work. It is a force that needs the refinement of work to be ignited.

Oliver looked up from the book from where he sat in his kiosk, he looked at the landmass that was the town. A great town unaware of its greatness or its untapped potential. He knew what the town needed, a touch. The town was like a canvas, awaiting the strokes of hard work to reveal its true beauty. Oliver promised to do his part in the painting.

He would become one of the men who through commitment, resilience, and diligence got the prize of success. He had read and heard of men who toiled diligently and made great stories out of the dregs of their life. He knew what he must do. The message echoed clearly—commitment, resolution and hard work are the keystones to unlocking the gates of purpose. And he had no intention of staying outside that gate, so he must work.

Oliver returned his attention to the book. As he continued to read, he felt a renewed sense of determination. The words became a roadmap, guiding him through the landscape of dreams and aspirations.

An instruction jumped at him, "Diligence also entails the wise use of your time."

It means a careful planning of time to ensure that the work to be done is prioritised. The diligent person makes sure the twenty-four hours of the day are milked till there is nothing left to do. It means giving the most important tasks on the to-do list the best of your productive time. A diligent person is a time conscious person, and a time conscious person will make a diligent person. It is an irrefutable law of success. Time must be planned wisely. Time must be allotted to every task. This will keep the frivolous use of one's time at bay. This will help one to number his days and apply the wisdom acquired to one's life. Time management is essential to the diligent man's success.

And so to Oliver's commitment to diligence, he must add a daily ritual of organising his moments, each second a stepping stone toward his destiny.

The final word was a resounding call for excellence; it lingered in the air, drawing his attention to it. He closed the book, the ember of diligence burning brightly within him. The embers that will birth excellence. Because wherever diligence is, excellence would be found. The sun outside seemed to glow with newfound potential, and the town of Evergreen felt like a canvas awaiting the strokes of a determined and diligent young artist.

Armed with the wisdom from these pages, Oliver closed the door of his kiosk for the day. He stepped into the bright and sunny day, ready to embrace the challenges and triumphs that lay ahead. The story of his season had just begun, and the pages of his life were waiting to be written with the ink of hard work and purpose.

# THE RHYTHM OF PERSISTENCE

The thought of persistence often took Oliver down memory lane. He would smile wistfully as he remembered the days of sitting on raffia mats under the night sky. The stars twinkling at him and his siblings, the birds on the nearby trees chirp happily and the cool evening breeze soothing and calm on their skins, while his mother told them stories.

Oliver's mother was the storyteller of the house, and it was a duty she gave all she had to. She managed to tell them a story at least three times in a week, no matter how tired she felt. Oliver remembered how she would inflect her voice several times during a story in order to capture the thoughts and words of her characters. Her facial expressions mirrored her character's emotions, and every one of her gestures told the story. She bodied the story and became one with her characters.

She wielded her stories like a soldier would his gun. Stories were her weapon, they were her tool and the means with which she correct a recalcitrant child. When a child needed to be encouraged, she used stories. When there was a warning to pass, she relied on the time proven power of stories to help her.

And it worked.

It did work, Oliver continued musing, because if it did not, why then was he here in his kiosk thinking about how the stories his mother told him about persistence had held and helped him in his journey and are still helping him.

She once told a story of a poor widow whose desire for help led her to a cruel and unjust judge. The judge's penchant for bribes and ruling in favour of people with the biggest gift was not hidden. He was a corrupt man that wore his corrupt badge proudly. It was to this cruel judge who had no regard for either God or man that this poor downtrodden widow took her plea.

She sought him out and closed her ears and her heart firmly to what people said about him. She knew his antecedents, but her will to succeed and the visions and aspirations of what that success would give her gave springs to her legs. So she went to this cruel judge and continued to go even when he ignored her. She appeared before him when he got angry at her insistence, and showed up when he warned her in words that would have scared a less resolved person. She persisted when this man humbly begged her and told her to desist from coming to his court. She kept going until the judge, tired and weary of her persistence, gave her the verdict she desired.

The whole town went agog with this woman's victory. Through sheer willpower and persistence, she had done what no one could do.

The lesson was obvious. Oliver remembered his mother had put it this way, "Persistence is the rhythm that gives life to people's creation. The only joy in the world is not just in beginning or creating; it is in the tenacity to continue, to keep painting even when faced with challenges. Every stroke requires effort, every detail demands perseverance."

Those words stuck, and they have been a great help in his journey. To his determination, he had added persistence. Against all odds, he would persist until his desire of becoming a successful businessman comes to pass. He would persist until his kiosk evolves into the big store he keeps seeing in his dream. He would keep knocking on the doors of prosperity until it is opened for him. Just like this poor widow in his mother's story, he would persist.

A chapter of the mystic book was titled, "Be Aspiring: High Expectations are Key to Everything"

The title struck him, he knew this would be a beacon for his ambitious spirit.

The great heights he envisioned in life must be directly linked to his expectations and aspirations. He could only go as far as his aspirations and what he expects from life. A high-flying life would only respond to an equivalent high aspiration

The book put it this way, "Know this profound truth; that aspirations breathe life into the human spirit. You should also know that those who fail to aspire begin to expire."

"Those who fail to aspire begin to expire." The words struck a chord in Oliver's heart, and he mulled over it in his heart until he came to a conclusion and made a vow to keep his flame of ambition alive.

He determined not to let his dreams wither away and embraced the concept that continuous learning is the key to avoiding stagnation. So, he would keep learning. He would let what he has come to know influence his aspirations, and he was sure the end result would be nothing short of an enviable and progressive future.

As he read, a proverb dropped in his heart, "The spirit of a man will sustain him in sickness, but who can break a broken spirit?"

He nodded his head in agreement at the truth in the proverb. A man's aspirations had the ability to give life to his spirit, it was a confirmation of what he read.

Oliver wrote the proverb in his journal and continued reading.

Then he saw another profound text that resonated with him, he understood it because he had lived it. The book pointed out the power of making use of opportunities, even the smallest ones.

Opportunities abound everywhere and in every nation of the world, the poorest inclusive. Another thing that abounds is people's inability to recognize and maximise these opportunities. Oliver concluded that these opportunities are missed because of the package they are encased in. Most are small, minuscule, and thus easily ignored.

A man with high expectations and aspirations will see these small opportunities for what they are worth and maximise them. When these opportunities are seen and recognized, the next step is to start, to begin. They are to start with the 'small' opportunities with the little that they have, in the small way they can.

His life was a living testament to the profound truth: "The only joy in the world is to begin."

However, he was quick to add that it is a joy that was not constrained to the beginning nor to the ultimate destination, it was a different type of joy. In the words of one of his mentors, "It is a joy that was not confined to the destination but scattered throughout the journey."

As he gazed through the vibrant weave of his journey, he found this to be so.

Oliver understood that every career in life was based on personal decisions. From the chapter of the book, it was instilled in him that anything he desired, dreamed, planned, and aspired towards, he could achieve. His success was not just about external factors but was deeply rooted in his will to succeed.

Where there is a will, there is a way to succeed. Where there is a man who believes in his abilities and capacity, there is unimaginable access to success. A man that would plan, is a man that would reach his goals. Aspirations give wings to everyone that aspires. Dreams come true to everyone who dares to dream. There really is no boundary to the high expectations of the man who chose to believe and speak great things about himself.

Speaking aspirations, beliefs, and desires into existence was another gem Oliver got from the chapter.

He wrote in his journal: "Speak what you want into reality. Make positive affirmations. Let the image of yourself that you see corroborate with the declarations you make."

So, Oliver made up his mind to affirm positive thoughts to himself. He would often say, "I am on top; I overcome all odds; I am born to rule." These affirmations fuelled his aspirations and set the tone for his day.

The affirmations pumped his resolve and reminded him of who and whose he was. It called to his attention that which was expected of his destiny. The more Oliver spoke, the more he believed he could become all that his affirmations said he could. His affirmations configured his reality.

When the author encouraged readers to pick problems and dreams bigger than themselves. Oliver took it as a personal challenge and wrote it down. He began to think about other projects and the opportunities he had seen in his hometown since he got back. He had delayed on doing due diligence by these opportunities because of the magnitude of what will be required to make them a success. Spotting opportunities was a responsibility, and he had shirked away from it, but not any more. He would do it. He would take on these bigger problems, just like the book suggested. From the chapter, he understood that by doing so, he would attract the support of others and accomplish feats beyond his imagination. Oliver determined that his story would become a testament to the power of aspiring and expecting great things.

He had since come to know that the difference between successful people and others is not a lack of strength or knowledge but a lack of will. Oliver's will to succeed became his driving force.

He would persist in these projects and succeed.

He would look beyond his current circumstances, low sales, lack of customers, and envision a great future. He would see beyond his limitations and not give up. He would affirm great things about himself, the projects, opportunities, and his journey. He would continue to learn so that his journey would not be beset by stagnation.

This was the way successful people lived, and Oliver chose to live that way too.

With his newfound perspective, he planned to encourage others to do the same. He would admonish them not to look down on themselves, to dream big, talk positively, and to picture a great future. Also, that starting small is only the beginning; it is high expectations and aspirations that propel people towards greatness.

# THE DANCE OF DETERMINATION

Oliver was not expecting his business to become an overnight success, that would be unrealistic, but nothing prepared him for the prolonged drought in sales.

The cartons that carried his goods were as pristine as the first time he brought them. The floor of his kiosk was clean on most days because no customers walked on them.

People walked past his kiosk and ignored his calls.

He applied the knowledge he had about marketing and for some time, it looked as if the sales picked up, but then it stopped.

Oliver was at his wits end. He spent most days in his kiosk wondering where he got it wrong. He thought of the rent of the kiosk that would soon be due. How would he get the money to pay if he was not making profit. He thought of things to change. Was there really a need to change anything?

Then he thought of the town and the supposed curse people said was on it. Could his lack of sales be a result of this curse? Had he bitten more than he could chew by coming back to the town to do business? Was there really a curse on the town, or was the supposed curse the hasty conclusion of people who had refused to stay and place a demand on their investment? Was it the hasty response of people who lacked the mental fortitude and strength of character to continue at a task until the desired result is achieved? Was he becoming a part of this throng of people?

Oliver sat in his kiosk and thought of all these as he saw customers walking past his kiosk without sparing it a glance.

Thinking was all he could do to stop himself from screaming and asking WHY ? WHY ME? WHY THIS?

Was there something he should be doing that he was not doing? He had a light bulb moment then. Strategies. "Definitely strategies," he said with the snap of his fingers, but the excitement did not last long.

It could not be strategies, he was way ahead of the other sellers in the market in terms of strategies. He had studied the people, the market and with that knowledge had tried to sell to them, but his results were short of expectations.

What else was he supposed to do?

Of course, he was not expecting his business to become a household name within a few months, but why was there no inkling of success? Why were his efforts not bearing the equivalent result?

Reflecting on this winding, ardent maze, Oliver was searching for answers through his trials, he wanted strength, he must find a way to embrace this weakness, he needed to turn the night, dark side of his business into day. In his deep thought, Oliver still felt a glimpse of hidden grace, a chance to learn what he must do right, a chance to rise and find his pace in this setting.

Oliver heaved a sigh of weariness and thought of throwing in the towel.

Perhaps it was time to give up the whole idea of transforming the town, of making a name for it by making a name for himself. Perhaps his dreams were too grand, he should probably give up and spare himself the headache. He thought of the people who had encouraged him. He thought of those who had placed their hopes in him, in the success of the business. How would he face them, he thought. But better their disappointment than this constant, annoying headache that his business was fast becoming to him.

Oliver stifled a cry and wiped off his tears with the back of his hands. He was looking for his handkerchief when his eyes fell on the mystic book he had been reading.

He picked it up reluctantly, praying he finds succour within its pages. He checked the table of content and found a chapter title Determination and opened to the page.

The chapter started with a question: What propels a person to be determined in the pursuit of their goals?

Oliver pondered and searched his own heart. He carefully examined the journey of his life. Were there times he had stuck to his guts and done what needed to be done in spite of the prevailing circumstances. If times like that existed, what influenced his decision?

Oliver kept pondering until the answer unfolded itself

"A clear vision of proximity to greatness."

Oliver saw that he stayed with goals because he saw what staying meant to the result he envisaged. He saw that staying meant success and greatness was within his reach. It was only people who stayed that are determined to wear the crown. Time and time again he had seen this play out in his life, so why did he think this time would be different.

Oliver realized that for him to get the result he envisaged in his business, there was a need for him to be determined. To work at his goal no matter what comes his way.

The definition of determination, Oliver learned, went beyond mere faith. It requires a complete faith—a mind and spirit resolute in achieving set goals. It is a force that manifested when one examined the conditions and challenges involved in the pursuit of greatness.

Determination is not something that can be stumbled upon, it is a character trait, a virtue that emanates from knowledge. Here, the determined person forges ahead, fully aware of the odds stacked against him. The determined person continues to do what should be done in spite of the challenges faced. In the case of Oliver, determination to him means coming to his kiosk every morning, opening its doors every day whether customers came or not. It means living every business day fully aware of the challenges that would come yet refusing to give up. And all this because of the pursuit of a specific result, in pursuit of success and greatness.

That is determination.

Determination emerges from a clear vision of aims and objectives. Oliver imagined a determined heart as one that had found something worth dying for—a profound purpose that light a fire within, urging one to strive relentlessly for their dreams.

Determination is not for the man beating the bush aimlessly, nor is it for the boxer beating the air. It is not for the soldier who wields a sword without an enemy in sight. Determination is not for everybody, it is for those who have a cause to fight. Determination is for those whose minds are set on an objective. It only works for people with an aim. It is people like this that would hold their ground and keep at their work until the aim or objective they have in mind is achieved.

The inference was obvious; determination is for visionaries. Determination is for people who know what they want and where they want to go. Determination is for people who are not confused about who they want to become. Tied closely to the apron of any determined person is vision.

The mystical book emphasised the importance of having a vision for the future, of making projections into the unknown.

Oliver reflected on his own dreams, he thought of his visions, then he reiterated that goals were seeds that needed nurturing. Goals are seeds, but they are not seeds to be cast without constant weeding and watering. Like a baby, a goal must be nurtured and cared for until maturity.

Thus, it must become priority to the determined person to guard against goal and vision killers. Dreams, like fragile embryos, requires protection from external threats.

Oliver was captivated by the story of Abraham Lincoln, a man who faced numerous failures but refused to quit. Abraham Lincoln lost eight elections and failed in business twice. Personal tragedies were a constant to him, at a time his health failed and he had a nervous breakdown. He was in the best position to give up. If he had, many would have empathised with him, and rightly so. Yet, he did not give up. He was resolute and determined. He bounced back from all his problems and went on to become the sixteenth President of the United States of America. The story of Abraham Lincoln's unyielding spirit echoes through time, revealing a man who faced failure after failure yet refused to surrender. Abraham Lincoln's story is a reminder that determination is the key that unlocks the doors to success.

As Oliver mulled over this story, he had an epiphany: a family's surname could be known worldwide through an individual's determination. Determination is one of the ways a man can stamp his name on the annals of history. He considered the legacies of Mandela, Obama, Awolowo, and others, realising that one's actions could immortalise a family name. These men, through their determination, immortalised their names. These were men who had every reason to turn back from the path of purpose. They were jailed for their convictions, and harassed for the colour of their skin. Poverty almost stopped others from getting to the peak of their careers.

Their stories swept through the corridors of possibilities, challenging Oliver to transcend the constraints of his family background and academic status. If Bill Gates, a school dropout, could rise to becoming one of the wealthiest individuals on earth, and if Obafemi Awolowo, who once sold firewood, could command respect in Yoruba land, Nigeria, then the barriers before Oliver were mere illusions. All he needed was determination. These men, whose stories now feed his heart, had one thing in common; they had a picture of the future and stayed determined.

As Oliver immersed himself in these tales of perseverance and determination, he wondered what his story would be. Would it be said of him that he gave up, or would history tell his stories of determination just like it told of these men.

These individuals, once unknown and unheralded, had etched their family names into the annals of history. The power of their stories, he realised, is not in their initial obscurity but in their unwavering commitment to their dreams.

Oliver embraced the mantra that winners never quit, and quitters never win. He recalled the inspiring words of Dr Martin Luther King, who lived and died for his dream, it was proof that a natural optimist could shape the course of history.

"What is it going to be, Oliver?" He said out loud.

"I will stand upon my watch," he answered himself, the words resonating like a mantra. He envisioned himself standing upon a tower, surveying the landscape of his dreams, and writing down his vision. For, as the words of wisdom continued, the vision was for an appointed time, and though it might tarry, it would surely come to pass. Oh, what a journey this will be! A journey that will be marked by a steady climb from deep shadows to peaks that shone brightly. Still in thought, he looked at his wristwatch to check for time. He was going to visit a friend. As he stood to leave, he muttered to himself, "I will walk the path of the unknown, yet I will grow in leaps, and bounds as seeds that were sown. I will be determined and not give up until my visions come to pass."

With newfound strength, he stood to his feet and embraced the call to believe in himself, to remain focused, and to be determined. The symphony of determination played in his heart, each note resonating with the stories of those who defied the odds. He understood that the journey to success was not a sprint but a marathon, where determination and unwavering belief would carry him across the finish line. A surge of determination course through his veins. The immortal legacies of determined individuals who refused to quit, fuelled his resolve. The dance of determination unfolded in his heart, a rhythm that he believed would echo through his lifetime.

# THE TAPESTRY OF CONNECTION

Oliver, buoyed by a new-found energy sponsored by his decision to work at his goals with determination, stood to his feet and began to walk around his kiosk. He walked the length and breadth of his shop, dusting this shelf and adjusting his wares. He expressed his recent resolve to be determined. Lethargy, the opposite of determination, is kinsman with hopelessness, he would not give in to it. From adjusting and dusting his shelves and goods, he went to the door of his kiosk and began to call on people walking past his kiosk.

His efforts yielded a customer, but Oliver didn't mind, he knew he would continue to do what needed to be done until he got the desired result. After the day's work, he closed the doors of his kiosk and took the path that led to his house. He was halfway home when he had a change of mind. The words from the mystic book had set a fire to his heart that he wanted to express. It felt like he would burst from the excitement if he did not share his new-found knowledge with someone. He had to talk, he just had to say something. He wished he could share with someone

His father's house where his siblings shout and scurry around while the younger ones seek his attention did not look like where he would get that kind of understanding companionship. So he turned back and took the path that led to Alexander's house.

Alexander has been his friend for two months. The friendship started from a good conversation, a rarity in Evergreen town. He had come to Oliver's kiosk for a purchase. His informed inquiries about the goods had caught Oliver's attention, and a long, satisfying conversation ensued from there. The friendship was sealed before the conversation ended. Several times after that time, they had paid each other visits. Visits that were crowned with great conversations and a promise of better days to come. Better days as friends.

Oliver met Alexander outside his flat, sitting on a long wooden bench, bare-chested and fanning himself with a raffia fan.

"The heat?" Oliver said as a form of greeting as he shook Alexander's hand.

"The heat is too much," Alexander concurred.

Oliver chuckled and went on to ask him about his day at work.

After some minutes of small talk, Oliver told him why he came. He told him how the lack of sales had gotten to him and made him consider giving up the idea of doing a business in the town. He was close to letting his months of preparation and work go to waste, but for the timely wisdom he got from reading the mystical book.

Oliver was expecting Alexander to throw in some words of encouragement and maybe tell him stories of successful people from the books he had read, but he did not. Instead, he laughed, a mirthless, dry laugh and said...

"And you believe that?"

Oliver looked at him, confused.

"These books have nothing to give you than great ideas that are unrealistic, and besides nothing works in this town. And..."

And on and on he went. Oliver watched him talk but heard nothing.

His bewildered mind went on a journey of its own. Did he come to the wrong house? Did Alexander have a double? Were their previous conversations a veil? How had he not realised that Alexander's beliefs were totally different from his? How had he called someone whose beliefs were far-flung from his a friend?

Oliver cut Alexander's tirade short and took his leave.

On the path that led to his home, Oliver realised that he and Alexander had had many conversations on many issues and topics, but none had centred on the things that really mattered to Oliver; like his goals, his vision, his business nor did they discuss Alexander's. They had spent all those hours talking, but not really saying anything.

Oliver's heart broke at that, he had been hasty in calling Alexander a friend.

At home, behind closed doors, Oliver brought out the mystical book and opened it, once again hoping for help and clarity.

The chapter titled 'Tapestry of Connection' seemed like the right one, so he read it.

There are two significant facets of connection. First, there is the physical connection which is an exploration into the realms of seeking assistance, whether financial, material, or moral. The second type of connection was the spiritual connection. This facet of connection has to do with tapping into the power to control your physical connection and bring them in harmony with you. Oliver pondered the synergy between the physical and spiritual, understanding that the alignment of the two was crucial in the pursuit of goals.

"Connection," Oliver continue to roll the word over in his mind.

Does connection also mean friendship? Is it a sort of relationship with the people in his circle?

The chapter clarified: Connection has to do with your proximity with the source of the materials or people needed in achieving your goals. Oliver mused over the truth encapsulated in those words. No matter the magnitude of one's goals, the key lay in forging the right connections. Connection, Oliver believes, meant friendship. It meant closeness to people who have his best interests and vice versa.

Having the right connection is an essential part of purpose fulfilment and goal achievement. Oliver realised that the people in his circle, the people who have access to him, could either make or mar his dreams. So there was a need to be very careful in the selection of his connection. His network of connection must be made up of people with like mind and goals.

Friendship is a matter of influence.

Oliver considered the impact and validity of that statement to the stories of his friendships and companionship on the journey to goals actualization. He remembered how his friendship with Maurice had changed his life. Maurice saw each day as a stepping stone to his great future. No day was spent idling away or on careless chatter. Every minute, every second was accounted for. He set goals and Oliver saw him achieve them. Maurice showed that success was possible. His life showed that efforts will always bring about the desired results, no matter how long it took. It was friendship with Maurice that stoked the fire of achievement that had already been built in him. He believed his dreams were possible because he had a friend who believed in him and also encouraged him.

Oliver reflected on Henry Ford's words, "My best friend is he who brings out the best in me," realising the significance of surrounding himself with those who uplift and encourage. Friends like Maurice, not Alexander, who talked down on his dream and discouraged him from seeing what he started to a great end.

There is a societal truth in Evergreen that tallied with Henry Ford's sentiment that a sheep that makes his home with dogs will act and live like one. Staunch in its assertion, this proverb carries the seed for profitable connections. Oliver used to be the sheep, the proverbial sheep who wanted to live out his dreams and make something worthwhile out of his life but nested in the dwellings of dogs. He had dreams, but it was a dream that would not transcend his relationships and friendships.

The wrong connections in his life are the weight that'll weigh down his ascension. For him to thrive, it is essential to break away from these unprofitable connections. Oliver did not realise how important this was to his growth, until he severed ties with friends who doused his fire.

When he pulled the plug on these connections, his eyes opened, and he saw his mistakes and others like him. People who complained of stagnancy in life, but whose friends were people who had no intention of living life beyond a certain tangent. These people with their mouths desired growth but moved with 'proverbial dogs' who made a ridicule of every attempt at change.

They spent days in religious houses and chased down mentors, when all they needed to do was to change the people they allowed in their circles. A person who believes that good success in business is possible should be friends with someone who believes the same. A student who believes getting good grades is cool should be friends with people who echo the same. Married couples who believe in the beauty of marriage should be friends with couples who extol such ideals. People who abhor hard drugs should be friends with people who share the same feeling. It is not discrimination, it is a strategy for winners.

All Oliver wants is to be a winner. He wants to win in life, win at his goals and all that his heart could conceive, and because of this he became intentional about his connections.

He had mentors like Professor Clinton, friends like Maurice. He needed more 'Maurice' in his life; friends who would help refine the treasure he carries, and a mentor like Professor Clinton who would give clarity and wisdom for his journey.

These were the VIP's in his life. They were the very important persons making sure his actions daily align with the future he wants. These very significant persons, friends in his life, are those assigned by destiny to assist in the fulfilment of his goals. They were his best friends because they understood his past, believed in his future, and accepted him in the present.

It was a friendship that went beyond familial ties or blood relations. Theirs was a bond sealed by unity of purpose and ideas. They were true friends.

True friends are pillars on the porch of life—sometimes holding up, leaning on, but always standing by.

True friends are always on the lookout, even if from a distance, for their friends. Nothing slips past them. They notice the pain and the anxiety even when no words have been spoken, and swing into action.

They provide a shoulder to lean on in times of trouble, and one is never left to walk through trials alone when they are there. They leave precedents with their track records and encourage the same in their friends. They motivate with their words and build up with their actions. Secrets are safe with them, and dreams are not confined to obscurity because of petty feelings of insecurity. They understand the tears and fears of the dreamer because they have been where he is or towing the same path too. They are all the motivation the goal-setter needs to achieve his goals.

Many dark paths had been lighted because of true friends. Goals accelerate because the goal-setter has people who care.

As Oliver read, he remembered the words of a wise man that a man who has friends must himself be friendly. Through this statement, he was reminded to be the kind of friend he wanted; purpose-conscious, goal-setter, motivator and helpful. He has to be these to his friends and to others in his path. When he does this, he would attract people of the same ilk to himself. It is a continuous cycle of give and take.

As Oliver journeyed through the wisdom of connection, he realised the importance of testing friendships and placing them in their best light. He contemplated the words, "You are the same today what you are going to be in five years from now, except for two things: the people with whom you associate and the books you read."

He came to understand that what becomes of a man and his future is closely tied to the friends in his life. A man's friend, albeit consciously or unconsciously, has a significant influence and can determine the similitude of his life.

In the quietude of that night, in his room, Oliver felt a profound sense of gratitude for the tapestry of connections in his life. He was grateful for Professor Clinton, the lecturer who called him son, at a time when he was in dire need of a father figure in his life. He was grateful for Maurice, who through sheer commitment to his goals showed him that his goals were not beyond actualization. He was grateful for Corper Josephine who taught with passion, mentored him from afar and heralded his return to academic excellence. He was grateful for Alexander because, through him, he was reminded of what friends are not supposed to be.

He heaved a sigh of relief as confidence in his goals returned, he was once again certain that he was heading somewhere, that his dreams were possible and that with the right connections, he would undoubtedly arrive at his destination.

# THE SYMPHONY OF WISDOM

Oliver sat at a vantage point in his newly expanded store and observed with glee the traffic that came and went from his store.

It was a far cry from what it used to be. His store was bigger, more beautiful and had become a centre of attraction. The walls had more shelves and the ones on the aisles had more goods. Sales attendants walked the length and breadth of the store attending to customers who it seemed were not tired of the store offerings. Who would have thought the town of Evergreen had that many people, most importantly, that many people with the purchasing power to buy what he sold. Who would have thought people could come from neighbouring towns to Evergreen to purchase goods? Such exponential growth in a town that had been nicknamed cursed. Such amazing business success in a town where businesses were doomed to fail before they even started. Oliver wondered at it all. Truly, the limitations of a man's mind are his worst enemy.

Oliver sat in his grand office and continued to watch from behind the glassy walls as people came and went. They came in droves, and they told the news to others that Oliver's store was the new best thing in town.

The story had changed. His story had changed.

Oliver continued watching, the buzz of conversation from the teeming crowd delighting him. As he watched and swivelled in his soft but overstuffed executive chair, his thoughts darted from his impoverished past to the abundant present. A change in times that had been wrought by the transformative power of wisdom.

Wisdom. Oliver's mind went on a solo journey at that word. His mind criss-crossed through times and years, till it stopped at the house of Pa Abel. He heard the word 'Wisdom' first from Pa Abel, the octogenarian who took a liking to him. Oliver tapped a finger thoughtfully on the large polished table where his fingers were spread and tried to remember where and how the friendship that set him on a course with destiny started. The relationship that put him on the path of goals, dreams, and purpose. His relationship with Professor Clinton and Maurice existed because of Pa Abel's gentle prodding, careful guidance, and thoughtful counsel.

Pa Abel was a revered deacon in his church, he had a thing for mentoring teenagers, and Oliver was one of the troublesome teenagers in church. His first contact with Pa Abel was the day his mother dragged him to his house so he could talk some sense into his head. That first meeting had been filled with long embarrassing silence, one-word responses, and pauses in between conversation that showed a lack of interest. Pa Abel must have taken it all in good strides because he sought Oliver out after that meeting.

And he kept seeking Oliver until the latter's resolve was broken. Everything melts before love. That was the sum of Oliver's relationship with Pa Abel. The conversations became better, and soon they were talking about everything, school, football, teenage crushes and Oliver's future.

Pa Abel asked him what plans he had for his future. "Fame, I want to be famous. I'll do anything to be famous." Oliver had blurted out.

Pa Abel smiled and then cleared his throat. He had turned to look at Oliver, smiled at him and cleared his throat again. He said nothing for a while, allowing the songs from the birds to fill the tense air between them that dark night

When he finally spoke, Oliver paid attention. There was a graveness to his words that commanded attention, it was the words of someone whose thoughts had been blessed by experience. Oliver did well to pay attention. He sat upright, straighter on the low-legged wooden stool and tuned his heart to listen

"That is the wrong way to go, Oliver. Seek Wisdom, it is the principal thing." He said.

That day, Oliver got it. He understood the assignment and applied himself to seeking the principal thing. His quest led him to books and mentors.

Whenever Oliver remembered the thirteenth chapter of the mystical book, he also remembered Pa Abel's counsel.

He found it amazing that he would find the similitude of teachings that Pa Abel had said to him years back in the pages of books.

Teachings that told him that wisdom was the key that unlocked doors. Some doors have remained locked because people have failed to acquaint themselves with the wisdom needed to open them. Some doors have been locked not because they were made from superior materials, but because the people made to open them chose to live a life dedicated to foolishness. It was never the door, it was them and their failure to apply their hearts to wisdom. Some problems have been unduly tagged unsurmountable because of a lack of wisdom. Wisdom remains the key that unlocks the doors to a fulfilled and purposeful life. When wisdom is passionately sought, success is assured.

This was a truth that Oliver wished everyone in the society would accept and assimilate. People would do all manner of things and search in different places for success, except in the right place; at the bosom of wisdom. Wisdom is needed for success in life, it is largely required to sustain success. There is a character trait and virtue that brings success and maintains it. That virtue is wisdom. The lack of wisdom has proliferated the society with people who are only as successful as their deep pockets. Money was all they had. A tragedy of a new phenomenon: poor rich people. People who had money but lacked empathy, grace, class, character, and the fear of God. They lived and swore by money, and see ungodly gains in business as being business smart. They are crooks in business, inflate prices unduly, gave and took bribes, and they termed it wisdom. In business, they sought money instead of impact. They would do anything and go anywhere for it.

Wisdom holds immeasurable value, incomparable to any material possession. It is an intangible force that ensures the possibilities of the tangibles. It is the powerful force behind innovations, and the reason problems get fitting answers.

The search for precious metals mirrored the pursuit of life's treasures—wealth, fame, and recognition. These pursuits are not necessarily bad in themselves, however they are cancerous in a heart that is filled with foolishness. The reason is simple. Without the companionship of wisdom, the desire for wealth, fame, and recognition could lead to disaster.

These desires become inordinate when wisdom is not sought and applied. Wisdom is the light that shines on the dreamer's path, it prevents mishaps and accelerates process. It ensures that the steps taken in pursuits of goals are within the circumference of morality. It ensures that the dreamer is not destroyed in his pursuits by his pursuits. Wisdom makes the pursuits possible, hence the reason it is placed far above material wealth. Nothing truly works without wisdom.

Wisdom will protect you from foolish mistakes in the pursuit of your goals, and where mistakes are inevitable, wisdom ensures it is minimal so it doesn't truncate the dreamer's purpose. Wisdom safeguards the earthly pilgrimage, and delivers from wicked conduct. It is wisdom that ensures that actions taken in pursuit of goals are bereft of destruction for everyone involved. Wisdom also protects the dreamer from the wicked conduct of others. It forestalls calamity by providing the mental clarity needed to scrutinise motives and actions.

Wisdom helps the goal-setter to stay ahead of the opposition. It is with the help of wisdom that a dreamer is able to reject alternatives offered by life, especially when the alternatives are injurious to the vision. Rejecting alternatives is often a prerequisite for success in one's goals. It is like when an athlete sets his focus on the mark and is not budged by distractions.

Oliver nodded in agreement as he continued to revere the virtue of wisdom. Wisdom is truly more precious than rubies, and it brings blessings to those who embrace it.

Just like it brought him.

There is a security that accompanies wisdom. It is a security that is contingent on putting into practice the good and the knowledge that one knows.

Wisdom, Oliver gleaned, is the key to an enriched life. It multiplies days and adds years. It is a gift that existed in the beginning, still is, and will continue to be. Wisdom is more precious than anything humans attach a price to. Wisdom is the compass guiding kings, governors, princes, nobles, and judges to rule justly.

Behind a well-governed country is wisdom. Behind organised and functional systems is wisdom. Wisdom is the sceptre of beloved kings and the bulwark behind the acceptance of nobles.

No wonder the wise man is always happy, it is a

happiness that stems from a place of lived benefits. The wise man is always happy because the profit from wisdom surpasses that of silver and fine gold.

As the verses of wisdom unfurled, Oliver felt the call to enter the house of wisdom, and to embrace reverence for God. The foundation of wisdom lies in honouring God continuously, a relationship that grants access to the mind of the divine regarding one's goals.

Oliver kept watching the activities in his store from behind the glass windows, marvelling at what wisdom had gotten him and where it had placed him. He said a silent prayer for the soul of Pa Abel and wished he was still alive to see what his admonition on wisdom had gotten his protégé. It was because Oliver sought wisdom that he was able to forgo alternatives and stick to the arduous but tested paths to achieving his goals. It was wisdom that made him choose values that do not contravene good conscience. He did not steal or cheat others in the bid to make a success of his goals, it was an attitude to life that wisdom taught him.

Oliver kept on watching and with a hand wiped off a tear that had slid down his cheek. His heart was glad, he remembered the decisions that had aided his growth, the things he did that had culminated into the future he is living. They were all offshoots of wisdom. His life and business had been built by wisdom. Wisdom had safeguarded his dreams and his life. He had found safety amid wise men with wise words.

Oliver stood from the chair and with hands folded behind him paced his office. As he paced, he imagined himself giving counsel to teenagers, to youths, to adults who were intent on writing great stories of their lives. He made a silent commitment to continuously choose wisdom and discretion. The mystical book had woven a symphony of profound truths, guiding him towards continual and great achievement of his goals.

"The blessing of wisdom belongs to the person who finds it," he whispered, allowing the wisdom-filled verses to linger in the air like a timeless melody.

# A MASTERPIECE UNVEILED

Oliver was ten years old the first time he saw a masterpiece. It was a beautiful work of art with an equally beautiful story behind it. It was a story that was the theme of most motivating speeches in schools and homes, and a point of reference for those who were daring enough to mention it in prayers for their children. When corrections in family homes turned to threats followed by a humble and sincere plea, the young boys and girls of the town were always certain of where it would end: the inspiring story of Benedict.

Benedict, a son of the soil. Their parents told stories of how they knew him as a teeny weeny child running about the town with nothing but panties with holes in them. They knew him when he used to walk with his siblings to the town's stream. They told of how he had a big appetite for food and many days had him outside his parent's house wailing whenever the food preparation took long. Some people even said his appetite for food was a pointer to what he would be. Surely, a boy his age with an appetite that big was bound to have an equally big appetite for life.

Oliver's father was one of the proponents of that appetite theory, and Oliver believed that must have been the reason he tolerated his almost unquenchable hunger for food. Many days he stared wistfully as Oliver ate, conscious of the price attached to it. Not only did Oliver have to contend with the fictional Oliver, his appetite for food also placed him in good stead as someone who could do for his family and his town what Benedict did.

Benedict, the painter and great artist, put the town on the map of the country and of the world. He left the town after his secondary education for a course in the university. He chose a field that was then alien to many and to the few who knew; a waste of resources. He chose fine art, and the success of his paintings and exhibitions justified his decision.

After years of tours and exhibitions, Benedict came back to the town where the seeds of his dreams had been planted. He came back to the town whose beauty had called out the creative in him. It was on this significant visit that Oliver saw his first masterpiece, but not immediately.

The news of Benedict coming spread like wildfire. Parents began to prepare their children for the August visitor. There were more counsels, more admonitions, more pleas. Teachers subtly wound his stories into their lessons. The prayers in religious houses became more direct.

A good number of them bought matching clothes. Shoes were polished until they shone, and children were cleaned and scrubbed until some bled. They did not mind that Benedict would only be seen by a select few, dignitaries who paid to watch him paint live in the town's library. All that mattered to them was that he remembered, from whence his rock was hewn. He had come to give the little that he had and also provide parents more fodder to first correct, threaten and then plead with their children.

After the live painting session which dignitaries from all over the country had come to watch, and a recorded speech that would be played in the schools in the town, Benedict's entourage left the town but his painting stayed.

The painting was taken to the town hall, where people who wanted to see it had to go in a queue.

Oliver joined the queue too. When he finally saw the

painting, he agreed unequivocally with others who had called it a masterpiece. It was. It was a canvas of colours and strokes that contrasted yet blended beautifully, its lines told stories, yet its beauty was simple enough to enjoy without the encumbrances of interpretation. To the uninitiated, it was clear as day and to the art enthusiast a beehive of meaning.

Oliver's ten-year-old heart swelled at the sheer beauty and power of this masterpiece, made by a man who was once a boy like him. A masterpiece that produced a masterpiece!

His mouth opened in awe, but his heart made a decision; just like Benedict, he would make a masterpiece of his life and the masterpiece of his life would in turn make masterpieces.

It took months of doubts, fears, and uncertainties, but Oliver did it. He made a masterpiece out of his life. Often times, he would stand at the riverbank of his life and peep into what his life had become. The masterpiece he had made of his life.

The once-blank canvas now told a story of beginnings, ambitions, unknowns, and persistence. He had also come to know the only joy in the world, the joy inherent in the act of creation, in witnessing the transformation of possibilities into realities. A possibility that showed that one could be anything they proposed to be.

Just like him, a wheelbarrow boy turned into a thriving businessman. The rain of abundance, promising a new fertile season, had triumphed over the formerly dry, unproductive season of his life.

All this because he made a decision.

Oliver knew something that most people who are masterpieces did not know. It was the knowledge that a masterpiece is always one decision away, a chain of events away from becoming thrash.

It is a secret he learnt from the seventh chapter of the ancient book that changed his life.

The title read, 'Never Despair, Keep Pushing On: Stay Focused.'

Masterpieces, in the euphoria of what they are, what they have become and what they have produced, often forget to put the grid of focus on their loins. They are quick to forget how their undivided focus on their goals, despite setbacks, had paved a path to success for them.

Oliver understood what it meant to be attacked on every side by problems, problems that looked like they were going to crush him and make mincemeat of the business he had laboured to build. He faced trials that were inevitable and encountered setbacks and disappointments of varied nature and magnitude, but he also knew and understood the importance of getting up each time. He knew the importance of setting one's face like flint and maintaining focus on the end goal. He had read and heard from mentors and speakers how being focused pays, so he chose focus above despair.

The mystic book also reinforced what Oliver knew, that the intensity of his focus would set the pace for his distinction in achieving goals. Focus would spur him on to action, not just knowledge. Focus is the key to success, without a strong reason or purpose, everything in life would be hard.

His journey was a testament to his strength in staying focused. The chapter likened persistence to focus and highlighted that persistence is the wheel driving dreams and goals. Thus even in the face of failures and difficulties, Oliver persisted, he remained focused because he understood that it takes the hammer of persistence to drive in the nail of success.

As Oliver thumbed through the book, he remembered the story of David. The face-off between young, inexperienced, war-naive David and the experienced, imposing giant that the Philistine Goliath, had for years served as a great example of what it meant to be focused.

The story of David's unexpected victory over Goliath did not start with the slinging of the stone, nor did it end when Goliath's head was off his neck. David's victory started when he maintained his stance that he could defeat Goliath, even when his brothers called him weak and his inquiries troublesome. He did not let that deter him, he knew what he could do and was focused on the result, he kept asking until he was taken to King Saul.

David's unwavering focus amidst distractions and criticism was his first victory. It accumulated into the victory that everyone saw: the death of the giant, Goliath. David's story inspired Oliver to fix his eyes on his goals. He knew that staying focused was a compulsory course in the curriculum for achieving dreams.

It also reminded him of one of his father's favourite sayings.

"When you get into a tight place where everything goes against you, and it seems as though you can not hold on a minute longer, don't give up then, for that is when the tide will turn."

Oliver has seen this play out so many times in his life. He has now made a mental resolution to not give up on any project, or business until he had done all that was humanly possible, and after that to try just one more time. After all, a little strategic crack is sometimes all a wall needs to come crashing down. In all his projects and endeavours, Oliver made it his duty to find that little but significant crack that would end hours and years of blockade, rather than throwing in the towel.

He had to, hence his masterpiece, which is his life,

will become thrash.

Oliver also realised that losing an hour in the morning could cost an entire day, a lesson he took to heart. This helped his commitment to his personal development, business, and projects. He made a decision not to miss any chances. This made him recognize that what seemed like the end was often just the beginning.

As Oliver's story unfolded, the town witnessed a transformation—not just in his life, but in the lives of those who had been touched by his journey. It was a journey his ten-year-old self who marvelled at Benedict's painting would be proud of. He did not become a painter, but he had become his special brand of masterpiece, unique to his gifts and identity. A masterpiece that had found expression through his personality and unique story. He did not become Benedict, but his masterpiece had produced and inspired budding masterpieces.

Oliver's journey continued, and with each passing day, the power of his focused mind became more evident. The town had a new hero, Oliver, but it was not because he possessed extraordinary abilities, but because he embraced the principles of staying focused and pushing on. He became a living testament to the idea that one could conquer not in brilliant style but by continuing, just as George Matheson once said:

"Success is possible with persistence and focus."

Thus, the young boy from the quaint town, armed with the wisdom from these chapters, continued his journey, inspiring others to start small, aspire for greatness, and stay focused on their dreams. Oliver's story became a beacon of hope for anyone ready to embark on their own path to success.

# THE DIVINE GPS

As Oliver walked down the street that led to his new and well-furnished flat, he thought of what he would say, if he were asked for the secret of his success. He wondered about the words to use that would adequately capture the tangible and intangible forces that made him the kind of person who could make goals, visualise a future, and employ strategies that made him a success. How does one statement capture that?

He could say it was his determination, his unflinching resolve to continue doing what he believed in, like making sure his kiosk doors were open even when sales came in trickles.

Or, he could say it was his ability to look fear in the face and defy it, just like he did when he started his business in a town where it was unanimously agreed that things never worked.

Perhaps he could tell the person it was his penchant for writing, and by that, not as an aid to memory. Writing for the sake of clarifying his objectives, his goals, writing so that light could shine on his weaknesses. He wrote to document his journey, a script of his success and the process.

He could say all these, and he would not even be lying or exaggerating the truth. However, his determination, faith, skills, and the virtues he had garnered over the years in his pursuit of reaching his goals are the glue that holds everything together. This glue is the secret ingredient that gave his efforts the needed glow, it gave speed to his feet and wind to his wings.

It is a GPS that was guarded and guided. It has carefully nudged him in the right directions. A divine GPS he thought he could call it.

At that, he sighed and continued walking. It was evening, which meant the greetings from passers-by were fewer, and he could dwell on his thoughts without unnecessary interruptions. He remembered a similar walk on a now distant date and smiled as he remembered his confusion on the said date, the emotional turmoil he was in. And how he could not wait to get to his favourite hideaway, under the shade of the oak tree. He wanted to put things down that would make sense of his life.

He had learnt that his goals were his life and his life was linked to the goals he made. This knowledge had pushed him to make goals and dream dreams that would give him the future he desired. He did everything within his power to reach his dreams.

Oliver waved a quick greeting to a passer-by and wondered the difference time and his goals had made. From that solitary walk to the oak tree to this solitary walk to his new flat were changes that his decisions had brought him. Changes that the Divine GPS had enabled.

Oliver looked up to the dark night sky and whispered a solemn and heartfelt, "thank you."

His life is proof of what is possible when a weak human acknowledges his weaknesses and avails himself of the power of a strong God. His life is a beautiful masterpiece of efforts and God's help.

Oliver asked God for help. In the journey to reaching his dreams, he heard stories of men like him, passionate and driven, who had made a wreck of their talents because they felt all there was to success and succeeding begins and ends with what their efforts could whip up. Their lives were the cautionary tales he needed to do things differently. And he did. To his efforts and strategizing, he added a plea for help to the One who could direct his path.

Oliver knew that seeking divine assistance was a key

to accomplishing and realising his goals. He knew he could not do it alone because there is a limit to what his strength could get him. He knew that to every success story and every dream that is reached, is the invisible hand of the divine. Oliver started out in his journey of purpose vowing to do things differently. He would not do it alone, so he asked God for help. His trust was in God, and he acknowledged His sovereignty over all aspects of his life, so he committed every goal into His capable hands.

When there was a deal to bc brokered, Oliver would often scrutinise the contract with his business knowledge and acumen, after which he would pray and ask God to help him. He acknowledged God by running his business in ways that were morally acceptable, like when he refused to give a bribe to one of his suppliers. The bribe would have meant the supply of more goods at discounted price. It would benefit the supplier and Oliver, but it would hurt the manufacturing company. He sold his goods with reasonable gain and never cheated his customers.

Oliver had heard it said that the world operated on different principles. It is said that success in business required a different language, that compromise is a thing, that cheating other businessmen and customers was necessary, that to succeed one must be ready to get his hands dirty and soiled. At the end of the day, the success that the world promised is built on the tears of the innocent and on a foundation of lies. It is a costly success. It holds no promise of lasting peace. Oliver did not want that. So he listened to the whispers of God. He allowed the Divine GPS to lead him in the right directions, and he learnt to ask for help before trouble came.

Oliver made up his mind to succeed in life, career, and business without guile. He would not lie nor steal or cheat and he would succeed. He believes that God had answers for every question, and he is the surest and most trustworthy guide in the pursuit of vision.

Oliver learnt that relying on human understanding alone was like leaning on a broken rod—imperfect and frail. So he flung himself into the hands of God, who could give him the understanding that he craved.

A wise man in one of his books admonished people to trust in God with all their heart and lean not or trust their own understanding. These verse gives a picture of the posture we must have with God. It must be the posture of a trusting baby with his parents. The baby cries because he is assured of being fed and taken care of by his parents. This is the kind of trust that we must have in God.

Another thing trusting God does is to choose a path for the one that trusts. Those who trust God and ask him for help, are automatically placed on a path that brings success without sorrows. Those who prefer success through illegal ways set themselves up for success with thorns that pierce and eventually kills. Oliver knew that the path he chose would determine his destination, so he trusted God and put himself on the path of success. That is good because it blesses the goal setter and everyone he interacts with. Oliver found out that doing things God's way in his quest for reaching his dreams, bestows courage upon those who walked in it, guiding them through the challenges that accompanies the pursuit of their goals.

Conversely, to ignore God's purpose is to embrace shame, failure, frustration, and destruction. Oliver remembered when he started following the divine GPS. There were times he would look over with a tinge of jealousy at the kiosk and businesses of people who had compromised their values yet were succeeding. It hurts to see them do crooked things yet go unscathed, but not for long; from his mentors, the books he had read, and the stories he heard, he learned that the world sometimes seemed to favour the wicked. It prospered those who cared little for righteousness. However, Oliver was reassured that God would turn their prosperity into ashes but would anoint the righteous, the one who trusted him, with the oil of gladness and restored the time lost in the wilderness of struggles.

That was Oliver's story, his struggles came to an end.

His business prospered. The big break came unexpectedly, he had gone to his kiosk with a heart full of hope, a determined resolve and nothing else. While he was cleaning his kiosk for the day's business, a middle-aged woman walked in. She looked like money. Simple, clean money. She spoke softly and kindly. Her perfume embraced rather than repel. Miniature lightweight earrings dwindled from her earlobes, and her gown was beautiful and modest. They exchanged pleasantries and as they did, he searched quickly in his mind for any whiff of recognition. There was none. She was new to the town. She asked for a particular product and for a brief moment, Oliver thought of doubling the price, that was what the other traders in the market did. She would not know. She looked like she could afford it, and he needed the money. Oliver shut down the thought as quickly as it came. Cheating was alien to his character, and not even lack of sales would change that. So he told her the price, the real price. The woman looked at him and smiled. A knowing smile, as if she was on to a truth that Oliver was oblivious of. Oliver wrapped her purchase in a fancy nylon and bid her farewell.

The next time Oliver saw her, she was in the company of other people, tourists who had come for a tour of Evergreen town. She was a tour guide who frequented the town but was unknown to Oliver. She was conversant with the gimmicks of Evergreen traders and had come to Oliver to see if he was like the others. Oliver proved her wrong and she became a lifetime customer. Not only did she patronise him, she brought tourists and recommended Oliver to traders and people in neighbouring towns looking for great wholesales and retail bargains. Oliver's integrity paved the way for him, his small kiosk metamorphosed into a big and thriving store.

As Oliver turned to the path that led to his home, the light from the skies seemed to dance with approval as he whispered his commitment to continue trusting in God. He would not lean on his understanding, but on the divine guidance that would illuminate his path toward the fulfilment of his goals.

His life had witnessed tremendous growth because he worked on his goals and trusted in God. His future was present, and his vision had become a reality. He is a different Oliver, now successful and purpose driven, and would keep succeeding and excelling because he had internalised the principles needed to excel in goals actualisation.

After years of careless living, Oliver found purpose, he reached his dreams, and got more out of life. Oliver looked at what he had achieved and the influence that had given him. He saw the beauty that his life had become and concluded that nothing succeeds like success. He flashed back to each setback and realised that they were breadcrumbs leading him to the feast. He smiled with a grateful heart and soul, for every part played and every given role.

He opened the door to his flat and he heard the whisper in his heart.

"What if you had not taken the chance?"

The answer wasn't a stretch, he's not so far from what he used to be. He vividly remembers what his life was before he took the chance to set goals that lead to achieving his dreams. He took a chance and the stars aligned in his favour. If you are reading this book, TAKE THE CHANCE NOW and watch the stars align in your favour.

# EPILOGUE

# BRUSH STROKES OF AMBITION

Oliver fought hard to keep his tears away on the day he opened his first store in a neighbouring town. He went through all the perfunctory activities in awe of how his life had turned out. Who would have imagined that the barrow boy of would turn out this successful. His store in his hometown is growing, and here he was conquering and expanding to other territories.

Oliver smiled at media men and shook hands with well-wishers as he continued to think of the masterpiece he had created out of the symphony of his life. His journey began with establishing goals and accepting the joy that comes with new beginnings. A new beginning that started with nothing but grit and determination.

He remembered the days of uncertainties. He remembered the day his fears weighed more than his faith and the nights he soaked his pillow with his tears. All he had were his dreams and ambitions that many had labelled unrealistic just because he dared to dare.

He questioned the belief that his town was cursed and challenge the conclusion that people born without silver spoons in their mouths were limited. He was the stupid son of the soil who had left a job and a new promotion in the city to come back to an uneventful town. He stayed and the story changed. He was no longer the stupid young man. Now they called him Guru and hail him as an expert on the streets. They said prayers for him for giving their sons and daughters jobs.

Oliver's story a demonstration of the power that may be achieved with perseverance, faith, and drive. His journey was not only a triumph for him personally, he believed it would be a worthy handbook for every dreamer and for every dream and ambition that exists within the magnificent fabric of creation. The lessons he learnt in his journey were a reflection of the universal fact that the process of goal setting was not only a pursuit; rather, it was a journey towards a purpose.

Through the ups and downs, Oliver has realised that the one thing that brings him joy in the world is starting something new. His dreams are standing tall, ready to welcome the second half of his life, and the canvas of his desires has been painted with the strokes of knowledge at this point. He's assured that things would keep on getting better for him, he knew he'd open more stores and create new ventures.

Oliver took the microphone that was offered to him and smiled at the small crowd that had come to felicitate with him on his new achievement. He reminded them of his story, his family background and how poverty had almost made a mockery of his ambitions. In clear, striking words, he told them of how adversities in the early days of his business had almost pushed him out of purpose. He had weathered all these challenges because of the heavenly hand upon him. This heavenly hand that is responsible for shaping fates and destinies had paved ways for him in difficult places.

Oliver shed a tear when he turned to look at where his mother stood. The stones on her native wear shone and blinked as the rays of the sun hit them. Her head was covered with an elaborate headgear. Her face beamed with satisfaction. She was happy and proud of his achievements. The woman that pushed the wheelbarrow from one door to the other is now the mother of a business tycoon. Oliver was happy too, but there was also a tinge of sadness, he wished his father was alive to witness the day. He wished his father was there to see how the seeds he had sown had germinated beautifully. He wiped his tears and gave a beautiful ode to his parents and siblings. He thanked them for not giving up on him, for their sacrifices, and their encouragement. He thanked them for helping him believe that he could rise above his impoverished background with the help of books, through diligence and innovation.

He told the crowd his success was not a solo journey, but of collective support that was always available in the hard and difficult times of his personal and professional life. He thanked his friends and mentors, Professor Clinton and Maurice especially, who also cheered him on. He acknowledged the customer who had helped him secure a job at the factory during his days as a barrow boy. He mentioned Corper Josephine, who reignited his passion for education.

Oliver concluded his speech by dedicating his new store to people who have faith in the possibility of second chances; those who have a strong desire for the second half of their lives to be more fruitful and satisfying. He told them that their dreams were valid. He warned them to be careful and not make a mess out of their lives by being impatient and unwilling to endure the process. He warned the youths and individuals who were running faster than their shadows of the impending disaster.

Oliver dropped the microphone after he told them

of his upcoming book. He had documented the journey that enhanced his personal growth, pushing him beyond perceived limits and shaping him through challenges. He believed it would be a book that would help young people realise their full potential. The words included within the pages would resonate with dreams, stimulate endeavours, and serve as a guiding light and inspiration. A beacon that serves as a reminder that every desire, every goal, and every joy in the world begins with the bravery to take the first step with boldness.

He now stood with pride as he reflects on the transformative period with deep resilience.

He quoted Francis Chan, 'Our greatest fear should not be of failure, but of succeeding at things in life that don't really matter.' He prayed that his story would serve as an inspiration to the people and encouraged them to appreciate the splendour of fresh starts and the boundless opportunities that present themselves.

Oliver walked away from the makeshift podium to the sounds of cheerful noise and applause. A well deserved recognition for a man who had defied all odds to chase his dreams, a courageous man whose actions had caused the stars to align in his favour.

# ABOUT THE AUTHOR

David Oyekunle is a seasoned professional in the tech industry, with a multifaceted career spanning nearly fifteen years as a project manager, researcher, business and customer insight analyst. A prolific contributor to academic literature, David has co-authored several peer-reviewed papers, solidifying his reputation as a thought leader. He is a member of the Project Managers Development Association of Nigeria (PMDAN), an affiliate of the International Project Management Association (IPMA).

In 2008, David published his first book, "Experimenting with Your Goals: 14 Basic Steps of an Achiever," which showcased his deep understanding of personal development and goal setting. His insights have been featured in leading publications such as ThisDaylive and The Guardian Nigeria. David's leadership and professional excellence have earned him numerous accolades, including the 'Excellence in Customer Management' award from Human Capital Management at Skyebank Plc (now Polaris Bank) and the 'Innovative Leader' award from the Lagos Central Baptist Youth Conference (LCBYC) and the Nigerian Students' Union UK (NSUUK).

David's passion for cultural exploration profoundly shapes his professional ethos. His extensive travels across Europe and Africa have enriched his perspective on diverse work cultures and management practices, which he seamlessly integrates into his coaching and mentoring programs. His biweekly newsletter, "Innovate or Stagnate," captures these global experiences and offers valuable lessons for professionals aiming to excel in a global business environment.

As a coach, mentor, and founder of Getitdone Consulting (UK); David has shared his expertise at numerous youth and leadership events, including those focused on the Sustainable Development Goals (SDGs). Beyond his writing and speaking engagements, David serves as a youth life coach and educational consultant with U&J Digital Consult Limited, an IT and educational consulting firm registered under the Corporate Affairs Commission (CAC) of Nigeria.

www.ingramcontent.com/pod-product-compliance
Lightning Source LLC
LaVergne TN
LVHW091328150826
845673LV00006B/1806

* 9 7 8 9 7 8 7 8 7 9 2 1 4 *